someone you know

a novel

gary zebrun

MANUFACTURED IN THE UNITED STATES OF AMERICA.

THIS TRADE PAPERBACK ORIGINAL IS PUBLISHED BY ALYSON PUBLICATIONS, P.O. BOX 4371, LOS ANGELES, CALIFORNIA 90078-4371. DISTRIBUTION IN THE UNITED KINGDOM BY TURNAROUND PUBLISHER SERVICES LTD., UNIT 3, OLYMPIA TRADING ESTATE, COBURG ROAD, WOOD GREEN, LONDON N22 6TZ ENGLAND.

FIRST EDITION: APRIL 2004

04 05 06 07 08  10 9 8 7 6 5 4 3 2 1

ISBN 1-55583-838-3

LIBRARY OF CONGRESS CATALOGING-IN-PUBLICATION DATA

ZEBRUN, GARY.

SOMEONE YOU KNOW : A NOVEL / GARY ZEBRUN.—1ST ED.

ISBN 1-55583-838-3

1. GAY MEN—FICTION. 2. JOURNALISTS—FICTION. 3. SEATTLE (WASH.)—FICTION. I. TITLE.

PS3626.E24S66 2004

813'.6—DC22   2003069506

CREDITS

COVER PHOTOGRAPHY FROM PHOTODISC.

COVER DESIGN BY MATT SAMS.

for Jim and Karen
and Chelsea

the slaughter

Seattle's Slaughter is like any other dusky leather-and-Levi bar anywhere else in the country—Ramrod, Dungeon, Outlaws, Studs—places where cigarette smoke mixes with the odor of sweat from so many T-shirted bodies. There's the smell of urine, stale and persistent, escaping from a doorless bathroom. At night, long after they have left their jobs, the men gather in these indulgent cellars. Their faces are shadowy and unshaven. Their smiles are mirthless.

I had decided that he didn't belong among these men. Even from as far away as the bar, where Slaughter's boy-bartender was handing me a Bushmills, the firefighter had the look of rescue all over him. He was sad and tender. Maybe intelligent. His face floated in the cigarette haze lit by the Mount Rainier neon sign suspended from the ceiling on chains. Smoke curled into a wing around his shoulder. As he picked up a cue stick from the wooden rail, he looked at me—long enough to see I was watching—before he turned on one leg, a kind of choreographed pivot. He bent over the table and leaned into it, his side forming a perfect beginning to an arc as he stood, lining up his shot.

"Make it three bucks," the bartender said. A silver Celtic cross hung from an ear. "Not much call for Bushmills here."

The firefighter waited a long time before he shot— a lightning strike against a solid-green ball, which was hurtled into the corner pocket. He remained bent over the table as he watched the cue ball stop a hair from where it had made its strike. His ass was firm inside his jeans. I noticed the clean crease his cheeks made in the soft denim. He was sizing up his next move.

When he straightened, he walked to the bar—close to me—where he chalked his cue tip and said, loud enough so anyone listening could hear, "I like the way you're watching me."

The music in the Slaughter sounded like sex. It didn't matter what song was playing: It all sounded like sex. Underneath it the DJ mixed a deep, insistent booming rhythm—electric and hypnotizing. At the far corner a small dance floor was cordoned off by a high chain-link fence that gave the room the appearance of a holding cell. About 15 men were dancing. Each one danced like he wanted to lose himself in the mess of bodies.

Everything important to me ceased to matter. My work didn't matter. My wife and daughter didn't matter. The mistakes and virtues that had defined my life didn't matter. In the Slaughter, they all disappeared into the smoky darkness. Surrounded by these men and their swarming desires, I believed only the firefighter mattered.

When he finished his game, he found me in the back room. I was sitting on a bench along the wall. It was the kind of block seating found inside a bathhouse, except the concrete was covered in dark-red industrial carpet stained with beer. The wall was painted black and lit by neon signs and a single strip of track lighting with two flickering lamps. The men beside me looked like coal miners resting against the wall of a cave. I imagined small round lights on their hats. Three lava lamps on a shelf across the room looked out of place, even sinister. They reminded me of bell jars from a circus freak show when I was a boy. My father had dragged me into the tent. The jars held deformed fetuses floating against the glass in a fluid that made their flesh look puffy and alive.

I leaned against the wall and fixed my attention on the men—about 20 of them—who stretched out beside me in the smoke. Some talked to the strangers beside them, others sat expectantly as they caught the eyes of passersby, some with a hand in a pocket, a few with a swagger. Here and there, like some tired Narcissus, a man stared down at the floor, painted black too, but polished to the glossy shine of a trooper's boots. I was one of these fags now and tried to imagine myself wearing a leather cap or vest, tight black gloves, a muscle shirt, chains, a harness, even a black leather hood. None of the gear suited me. I wore a white shirt and khaki trousers, scuffed brown loafers. My tie and tweed jacket were in the car. A few men had on lumberjack shirts, but everyone else, except for me in my weary preppiness, wore Levis, leather, and T-shirts. I unfastened the top buttons of my shirt.

The firefighter appeared and asked, "So what are you drinking? I want to buy you one."

"It's a Bushmills—Irish whiskey on the rocks," I said.

He winked. "I know what Bushmills is."

I wanted to believe his wink was reassuring, maybe a gesture to help me feel at ease. But he was flirting probably like he'd flirted a hundred times before.

Besides his blue jeans, he was wearing a navy blue T-shirt with the name of his fire station—DEFIANCE ENGINE 5—on the back. He looked 30-something. He had thick brown hair, short, a little higher than an inch—sculpted uniformly on the top, back and sides. His sideburns were trimmed close and almost level with the bottom of his ears. His ears were small and delicate, his eyebrows substantial. He wore small oval glasses with a thin tortoise-shell wire frame that gave him the look of seriousness I'd noticed when he was playing pool. He turned to get my drink before I could see the color of his eyes.

While he was at the bar, an older man sat beside me. He was wearing black jeans and a black leather vest open from his neck to his stomach, where it buckled shut above the waist. He had thick, gray hair. Patches of fur covering his chest were white and wiry. A pair of clamps hung from his nipples on a silver chain and reminded me of miniature jumper cables.

Every once in a while he touched one of the clamps and pulled it out, making his breast look like the kind of thing I'd seen in comic book pornography. He moved his leg against mine and flexed it against my thigh. He didn't look at me. I thought of standing somewhere nearby and sending him a look that would make him feel like pond scum. But I stayed seated and stared at the black floor and watched his leg pulse against me. The desire I'd felt coursing though me all night in the Slaughter disappeared until the firefighter returned with my whiskey. The older man shot him a look and walked off.

"You don't look Irish," the firefighter said, handing me my whiskey.

He smiled, lifted his beer—a longneck Rainier lager—and said, "Here's to a good Killarney mist. I'm Stephen Hart. You're not from Seattle."

"Right. I love the Irish for their whiskey and poetry. I'm from the other coast, from Providence," I said.

"I've been there. At an EMS convention on rescue equipment: defibrillators, portable Jaws of Life. That stuff. I liked the way the river runs through the city. All the colonial houses on a hill. Cozy gay bars. I don't read much poetry."

"You're a fireman."

"We're awfully popular these days."

I didn't know what else to say, and I worried my silence was insulting.

"So you're here in the city of the Space Needle with the queen of the Slaughter, and all you can tell me is I'm a fireman." He laughed and patted my leg.

Then, after a pause, he said, "I don't think you're a snob, at least not yet."

He sat beside me in the space the nipple-clamp man had left. "What's your name?" he asked.

"Daniel Caruso." I held out my hand, as if meeting someone to interview. He was surprised but accepted it. His handshake was strong.

"Like the singer?" he asked.

"No relation."

I was afraid that if I said anything else he'd walk away.

"You don't look Italian. I guessed German, maybe Polish." He touched my shoulder and said, "These big bones don't look Mediterranean."

"I resemble my mother's side of the family—Russian—but I feel closer to the Italians."

"That's good." He ran his hand halfway down my back.

"I think so too. Every once in a while I can brood like a Russian, but mostly I like things livelier."

"Let's see. You have a son and a daughter." He rested his hand on my knee.

"Who said I was married?"

He touched my wedding band. Then he spread out his hands, palms down, as if ready for a manicure, and putting on the fey, he said, "See, I'm single, both ways."

"And cute," I said.

"I bet your kids would be astonished to see you flirt with a guy."

I was surprised he'd said "astonished." *Maybe I really am a snob,* I thought.

"Just one daughter. She's going to college in the fall."

I didn't want to think about Jamie or my wife.

"So flirting comes pretty naturally for you. What's Hart? Irish?"

He looked like he had to think before answering, and said, "I'm a mutt, but lots of English. How old are you?"

"Forty-two," I said.

"You look pretty good still—must be the olive oil. I'm 39, but I'm told I look boyish, which helps."

"Helps with what?"

"With…" He hesitated. "With just about anything, honey. Except tonight. I had to buy you a drink."

"I'm glad you liked me watching you earlier."

"It was kind of sexy."

I could tell that he'd talked like this to other men before. I didn't care.

"I liked the way your ass filled your jeans when you leaned into the table," I said.

"You're pretty bold for a daddy."

I touched his knee with the tips of my fingers and moved them up his thigh, pressing them against the soft denim. It was intoxicating.

"You should know what you're getting into here. The Slaughter's no place for a novice," he said.

He leaned over and kissed me—a deep, satisfying kiss that made my skin tingle. He breathed into me and sighed. He closed one of my eyelids and I felt the gentle pressure of his lips upon it.

He whispered, "You'll do just fine."

■

The firefighter lived in the third-floor apartment of a painted Victorian lady on a sloping street that overlooked Volunteer Park. I followed behind his sporty Isuzu Trooper with the license plate BLAZE26. Before turning into the driveway, he stopped, stuck his head out of his window, and told me to park along the street.

Other men had taken me home late at night when almost everyone else in their neighborhoods had darkened their houses and gone to sleep. I never stayed until morning because I'd convinced myself that waking up beside a man in his bed would take me to a place where I could never turn back. And turning back was what I'd learned to do better than anything. A brief encounter in a hotel room, bathroom, or park had always been a diversion, a kind of temporary stay against the truth. I had a wife and daughter, a career. I'd accepted this big lie. But that night I decided, without any of the usual hesitation, to step beyond my limits. I would not leave Stephen's apartment until the sun rose out of the Atlantic, slung itself over Rhode Island and eventually lifted the veil of darkness from the Northwest.

He met me at the bottom of his driveway. For a moment, in the lamplight, he looked like all of the men I might have ever loved.

"Down there." He pointed to the trees and lit paths of the

7

park. "If you listen closely, you can almost hear tricks rustling through the shrubs."

I thought he said "ticks." But then I knew what he meant.

Beyond the park, the moon, golden, hung over downtown Seattle. A wispy line of low clouds was gold too, fiery, as if the clouds were lit by a carbon arc lamp, the kind of flame in an old movie projector. Above us, over Capitol Hill, stars made thousands of white flecks in the sky. Stephen reached his arm across my back and cupped his hand around the side of my butt.

"Some nights I think there must be a hundred men scratching their way through the bramble to a clearing of lichen and ferns," he said.

"You've cruised in the park?" I asked.

"A few times. But usually, I like to see what's in store for me."

"It isn't safe."

"Risks are just the beginning. It's what happens afterward that counts."

I wasn't sure I understood, but I didn't want to take the time to think about it because I was afraid I would leave.

"It's got to be lonely there," I said.

"Ask the guy on his knees in *that* chapel. I'm not sure he'd say he's lonely now."

He took my earlobe between his lips and breathed on it.

I said, "Once, at a rest stop on the highway outside Providence, I slid through an opening in the chain-link fence and followed a path into the woods. Men were stationed, like sculptures, beside trees and in corners of thick brush. Tissue papers and condoms were scattered over leaves and pine needles. One of the men faced me. He was playing with his cock. I tripped and ran. When I got back to the car, I was shaking."

"You're pretty steady now." He touched my crotch, softly.

"This is different," I said. "I like you. It's not so fucking anonymous."

I almost said monogamous.

He whispered, "Everything's anonymous."

"You sound like Sartre," I said.

"What the fuck is Sar-tra? Some Eastern religion?"

"He's a writer, a French writer. He's dead."

"I don't care who I sound like, as long as you take me somewhere sweet tonight," he said.

As we walked up the driveway he kept his arm around my back. And he was right. Behind me I could almost hear the tricks rustling the brush.

■

His windows were covered in wide, slatted blinds—white and wooden—with no curtains. The blinds were open, and through the slats I saw the lit paths of the park. There were two large silk screens in corners across from each other at the back of his living room. They each depicted a Tahitian scene—Polynesian men and women painted in wild colors on a backdrop of a rain forest, like a Gauguin. Along one of the walls, over a stylish Japanese couch, a row of Mapplethorpe's photographs: nude black men curled into rock-hard poses. In the center, larger than the other photos, a white cross with a wide black border.

There was bric-a-brac everywhere: a model of a small aquamarine-and-white motel somewhere on Southern California's Route 66, with a pink Volkswagen Beetle parked outside it and a palm tree stuck into a tiny patch of artificial turf; beside that was a hook-and-ladder truck, bright red with shiny chrome details, its ladder extended into the air. In the middle of a glass coffee table was a *Simpsons* chess set, with miniature Barts and Homers and the rest of the characters lined up across from one another on teal and yellow squares. On a shelf beside a row of *National Geographic* magazines was a plastic statue of Frank Sinatra in a suit and fedora and Elvis Presley in tight black pants. The two pop idols faced each other with dueling microphones at their mouths. An inflated Betty Boop hung from the ceiling. Inside a crystal bowl below her was a pair of handcuffs.

Stephen noticed me looking at the handcuffs.

"The whip and chain are hidden in the closet," he said.

"I didn't think you'd be into bondage."

"I'm kidding. I thought the cuffs inside the family crystal made a statement." He smiled and said, "I've got the key somewhere if you want to try them on later."

"I think I'm passive enough without them."

He pulled me against him and patted my ass with his hands, lightly, again and again, as if he were keeping beat to a song.

"I'm in the mood for a passive man tonight," he said.

He slid his fingers along the crease in the seat of my khakis. "I like this," he said.

I felt the pressure of his fingers, first the strong index finger, pressing inside me and finding the opening he wanted. He pushed the soft cotton of my briefs inside it. I didn't think, *He's a stranger. What am I getting into?* His touch felt lovelier than anything I'd imagined.

"How about some Louis Armstrong?" he asked.

"Nice," I said. But before he turned to put in the CD, I kissed him, first on his lips, then his chin. I kissed the center of his T-shirt and felt thick chest hair beneath it. I knelt before him and pressed my lips against the center of his jeans, working back the strip covering the buttons and breathing into the denim, long and warm breaths. I could feel him getting hard against my face.

He had placed his hands on my head.

"You keep surprising me," he said. "But understand one thing: I run the fuck."

He turned away to put on the music, leaving me there still on my knees.

I moved to the couch and listened to the sound of Armstrong's horn filling the quiet Stephen had left me in. I was glad there were no lyrics to distract me. "Keyhole Blues" was like the night itself: a clear acceptance that nothing simple would ever happen again. Lyrics would have told a more hopeful story. Or a more woeful one. Words usually exaggerate. The music of the trumpet knew better.

He placed two beers on the glass table next to the Simpsons. He sat and took my hand. I felt an unexpected tenderness.

"Why are you here?" he asked.

"I think it's chemical," I said. "You stunned me into wanting to be with you."

"I mean in Seattle." He slid his thumb along my palm.

"It's business."

"You're secretive. It's a little scary."

"I'm a columnist for a newspaper. I've been here all week at a forum on writing. I gave a lecture a couple of days ago called 'Confessions of a Liar: What a Columnist Tells and Keeps to Himself.'"

"I know a reporter. They're not as honest as you'd think," he said.

"Sometimes a columnist needs to play the confidence man," I said.

"What's that?"

"It's a liar, maybe worse, because a confidence man

11

makes an art of gaining someone's trust before he abuses it."

"So I shouldn't trust you."

"Most of my lies don't end up in my columns."

"So am I going to be in a column next week?"

"You're a secret."

"A dirty little secret."

"No."

He looked at me as if I were someone he'd known long before that night. Armstrong played his horn so sweetly, I wanted to melt into Stephen's lap.

"Do you like dancing?" I asked.

"This is awfully sleepy music," he said. Armstrong was playing "Melancholy."

I knelt before him and removed his shoes. I pulled him from the couch.

The rest of the night he called the shots. He undressed while I sat at the edge of his bed and watched. His chest was muscular and hairy, and a dense patch of hair circled his navel. The muscles in his thighs were statuesque. His balls and penis rested snugly inside his cotton shorts. When he pulled them off, his sex fell softly down from a thick tuft of dirty-blond hair.

He stood in the light from the hallway. Then he pulled me from the bed and kissed me. He took my hands and drew them behind him and rested them on his naked ass.

"You're next," he said.

"I think we should have that talk about our sexual histories," I said.

"You don't have to worry about me. I'm no confidence man."

"But I was born worried."

"Born yesterday, you mean. I'm going to use a condom when I fuck you. Besides, I'm negative. How about you?"

"I've never been tested, but I've also never been fucked."

"Then you've got a sweet surprise ahead of you."

I kissed him and said, "I usually don't like surprises."

For a moment I remembered Sarah and Jamie and considered stopping. I thought, *He's a stranger. What am I doing?*

"So tell me about your lovers," I said.

"Shit. What do they have to do with this?"

"More history. You know I'm married, with a kid. I haven't fucked. What about you?"

"You want to know how many times I've fucked? Let's say Willie's a celebrity."

"No longtime lover?"

"This is a first date. Why the interrogation? You don't want this moment to slip away."

He looked down and seemed embarrassed, maybe even nervous. I could tell he wasn't as promiscuous as he pretended to be. Then he surprised me.

"That *Simpsons* chess set out there—Sam gave it to me about five years ago. He's a reporter, too. Crime beat. Married, just like you. After about a year he started to knock the crap out of me. I loved him—sometimes I still do, but he's bad news. Not gentle, like you seem, not even in the beginning. He stopped seeing me almost a year ago the day after he broke one of my ribs with a fireplace log. I told him I'd go to the cops and his family if he ever stepped foot in here again. Happy, now that you know too much?"

"I'm sorry," I said.

"You ever hear Magnetic Fields?" he asked.

"I hated physics."

"It's a band, all queers: 'All the things I knew I didn't know/And didn't want to know.' "

"I don't get it."

"It's one of their songs. It's like I'm saying: You think too much."

"Right."

"You still want that surprise?"

I nodded, and he unbuttoned my shirt, which fell to the floor. He pushed me, gently, back onto the bed and knelt to take off my socks. When I touched the small round bones that ran along the middle of his spine, I thought about him being hit with the fireplace log. Then all I thought about was his nakedness. He pulled me up and unbuckled my belt and pants. He unzipped my fly and pulled off my khakis. He knelt again and pressed his tongue into my navel, removed my briefs with his teeth. He licked the spaces between my balls and legs.

All through the night Armstrong's trumpet played the same blues over and over. What happened from this point on was filled with the trumpet and the night. What I tasted of Stephen was shadowy and spectacular. When he entered me, the pain and wonder of him moving inside me irrevocably changed everything.

"No one has ever entered me there." I knew I'd repeated myself.

His only response was a melancholy sigh, which might have been, I couldn't tell for sure, notes from Armstrong's blues.

■

I was awakened by a slash of sunlight across my face. Stephen Hart wasn't lying beside me. I couldn't hear him anywhere outside the bedroom. I'd stayed through the night with a man in his bed and wanted to believe what had happened would mark a beginning. I wanted to put my arm around his side and rest it across his stomach. I wanted to tell him I was sorry about Sam and maybe, if he wanted to, we could meet again sometime soon. I imagined a beach in Costa Rica. A hotel room near Central Park. A cabin in the Rockies. The sunlight on my face felt like a rebuke.

I slipped on my shorts, which were on the floor next to the bed. He wasn't in the living room or the kitchen. The bathroom door was open. I saw a note taped to the mirrored wall: "Daniel, I went to the station and didn't want to wake you. Thank you for last night. It was fucking beautiful."

The note was signed Stephen. No "love," no "call me sometime," no X's and O's, just Stephen. I pulled it off the mirror, returned to the bedroom, and lay on my back in his bed. I held his note against my thigh, and thought, *Fucking beautiful?* My ass hurt. I remembered it hurting last night, too, while I spooned against him. He'd fallen asleep long before me. I'd listened to his breathing and tried to sleep to its rhythm. I remembered his condom breaking while he was pushing himself deeper in. I could feel him, warm and slippery inside me. I wondered whether my wife felt something mysterious like this when I left a part of me inside her. Alone in his bed, I thought I could still feel his cum. *Why aren't I worried?*

I took off my shorts and stepped into the shower. There was no soap. I stepped out and looked on the sink. None. I opened the medicine cabinet and saw a prescription bottle of pills with the faded letters AZT printed on the label.

He'd told me he was negative, and I tried to convince myself I could count on his honesty. My flight to Providence was leaving in less than two hours. I thought about home and trembled at what I'd done so far from it.

I jumped into the shower and ran the hottest water I could stand. I turned my back to the showerhead, and bending over,

15

I opened myself to let the hot water cleanse what it could. My ass burned but I didn't turn away.

I dressed fast. When I left the apartment, the door locked behind me. I wondered how I'd reach him. He'd have an explanation. What was the name, I thought, of his fire station? Then I remembered DEFIANCE ENGINE 5. I thought about a reporter named Sam. I felt unsteady and leaned back against the door. Volunteer Park in the morning light looked green and harmless. Its furtiveness was gone. I felt sick.

On the way to the hotel for my luggage, I saw how easily chaos had happened, how a single night had stolen more than just the measure of caution I'd lived on for so long. I was angry, terrified at what might have been let loose inside me. I knew it would be a long time before I'd have any idea how to put my life back together again once it finished unraveling.

At the hotel there was a phone message from my wife. Her voice sounded content and happy. It hurt.

It's late. Are you out getting soused with all those egomaniacal writers? We miss you here. Night. Love you, more than I should. And don't forget to bring home some Dungeness crab.

good friday

From the air over Wyoming the Grand Tetons looked brown and blasted. I leaned against the window and listened to the hum of the engines and a hiss from the small air jet above my seat. In the row ahead, a man was reading magazines: *Harper's, Money, Newsweek, Golf, Esquire, The Atlantic.* He snapped each page when he was finished, reading fast—*snap, snap, snap.* I couldn't sleep.

The flight had left Seattle late because of fog, and by the time the plane neared Chicago, it was dark. Specks of light appeared as we descended—sodium arc lamps along roads, clusters of house lights in suburban subdivisions, flood-lights in parking lots, streams of car headlights. It was a landscape flickering in vigil. I pictured Stephen Hart fucking me, and I thought, *Nothing good will happen to me for a long time.*

On the empty seat beside me was the front page of the *USA Today.* The hit for the day—Good Friday—featured a village in the Philippines that reenacted the Crucifixion. Jesus was played by a young Filipino—a boy really—who was nailed to a cross. Blood dripped from his hands and feet, where other villagers had driven in the nails. More blood covered his face from the small wounds beneath his crown of thorns. The headline was EXTREME RITUAL: FAITH AND VIOLENCE. The young man's expression was anguished and exalted, his chest hairless and oiled, his nipples large and full, as if the pain had aroused him. He was handsome.

The woman in the aisle seat next to me looked at the newspaper.

"It's a bit much, isn't it?" she said.

"A fanatic," I said.

A few minutes later our plane touched down at O'Hare.

My flight to Providence was delayed for hours because of thunderstorms and tornado warnings across the Midwest. I hadn't eaten anything all day and wasn't hungry. I thought about looking for a quiet corner near my departure gate where I could start Sunday's column, but I didn't have an inkling of what I was going to write about. HIV and AIDS and AZT, the letter-words streamed across my mind. I wasn't going to write a tell-all that would begin: *Yesterday a firefighter fucked me and changed my life.*

I didn't want to think of what would happen next. *Exhaustion,* I thought. *It's dangerous to face any crisis when the body and mind are shot.*

I decided to walk around and passed a bank of telephones and remembered to call home. My daughter answered.

"Dad," she said, "why aren't you home?"

"I'm stuck in Chicago," I said.

"'Does anybody know what time it is?'" she asked.

"'Does anybody really care?'" I said. She liked to sing

stray lyrics of songs from my high school era. It was a game she played with me.

"I've missed you, Dad," she said.

She made me feel guiltier than I'd felt before.

"Mom dragged me to the Stations of the Cross and cooked fish for dinner. She said she wanted to see how she'd respond to religious sorrow. She used those words: *religious sorrow*. I thought she was out of her mind."

"Where is she now?"

"So much for religious sorrow. She's at the Cable Car with Julie and Annette; some old film about a lesbian called *Chasing Amy*. I bet they go out for burgers."

"Did you like the Stations?" I asked stupidly.

"What's to like, Dad? People nailing a man to a cross. I think I prefer Zen."

I laughed and said, "I love you."

"I know. It's sick. Dads are supposed to be frustrated with their daughters by now. It's part of the letting go."

"You're too much like your mother."

"That's it. End of conversation." She pretended to be prissy.

"Things would be empty without you," I said.

My seriousness surprised her.

"What's wrong today? First, Mom drags me to a crucifixion and now you're talking all gloom, too. Are you OK, Dad?"

I'd heard this note of worry creep into her voice recently, as if our roles were slowly reversing. I was afraid of hurting her.

"I'm fine," I said. "Bad flights make me moody. Hey, did you ever hear of a group called Magnetic Fields?"

"Never. They sound kind of punk. Why?"

"Someone mentioned them, and I knew if they were

anyone, you'd know. Tell your mom I'll be home late, probably after midnight. Don't wait up."

"You won't find me awake. But do me a favor: Check in on me."

"I always do."

"Cool, Dad."

"Bye, kiddo."

She started to sing "Bye, bye, Miss American Pie," and then hung up the phone.

I stepped onto a sliding walkway and felt as if something elemental in me, something unidentifiable but essential, was evaporating. I thought about Stephen Hart's cock inside my ass. It felt spectacular. I thought, *I have to stop lying to them.*

The walkway ended, and I stumbled off, bumping over a suitcase that a woman ahead of me was setting up in a collapsible cart.

Gray, hairy dots lumbered across my vision. I knew I wouldn't faint, though I believed I could just lie down and curl into a zero on the cold floor at the mouth of the walkway where everyone else was stepping off.

Three nuns in black habits passed by and nodded soberly, aware I was watching them as they headed for their flight. They were accustomed to the attention, and I was disappointed their nods were so neutral. Their habits billowed like three sails of a schooner tacking close to shore.

A man called out to them and they waited. He had thick auburn hair and a beautifully chiseled nose. Maybe he was a priest—40 years old, no more. I thought, *He's handsome.* I couldn't stop myself.

Two young men dressed in Army camouflage pants and shirts and carrying automatic rifles stood near a security checkpoint where travelers were passing to their gates. The guardsmen reminded me of a picture of my father in his boxer shorts, huddling with his Army buddies—all dressed in boxers—as they looked unselfconsciously into the camera lens that caught them outside their barracks on a hot Texas afternoon in 1944. Their faces were boyish, not at all embarrassed. They were laughing. I used to imagine hanging with them, dressed in white boxers, too. At first I wanted to pretend I hadn't seen it, but soon I waited all day for the night, when I could look at it alone before I slept. I had hidden the photo under my pillow even before my father left the house for good. When my mother found it one morning, she thought I'd kept it as a reminder of him. She didn't know I dreamed of going into the barracks with his buddies after a long day in the Austin sun, stripping and showering. She didn't know I wanted to be happy like the soldiers.

A guardsman walked up. "You OK?" he asked.

He must have seen me stumble into the woman with the cart and wondered what I was doing just standing there.

"I've been in airports ever since the morning. I guess I'm beat," I said.

I could tell he didn't think I was a threat, not even worthy of some low-level concern. He just wanted me to get on my way.

"You can't stand there," he said.

"Right," I said and walked to my gate.

The waiting area was quiet. Men in suits slumped in chairs, talking softly on cell phones or reading newspapers or reports. There were sleepy students headed home for Easter—some of the girls reminded me of Jamie. I thought, *Sometime soon I'll be a "he" to her and not just Dad. She'll be alone with her mother in the house, and she'll say, "I'm sorry he hurt you."*

It was 9 in the evening. On a television across from our

gate, CNN showed footage of twisters that had touched down in Omaha and Cedar Rapids. The worst had hit farther north in a little Minnesota lake town called Nebish. A waitress from the Buena Vista Diner described for a reporter how she'd ducked under the counter and wrapped herself around the iron base of a stool when she heard the wind begin to roar like a freight train. "I read somewhere," she said, "you're supposed to hug something bolted down. So I just made a date with the stool."

Almost apologetically, she said again that the twister really sounded like a freight train and she wished she could find a fresher way to tell the world about it. She was pretty and spoke with a girlish voice. She fixed her hair while she talked and flirted a little with the camera. Behind her, the roof of the diner was torn back like the metal lid pulled halfway off an anchovy can. Tables and chairs were splintered. A ketchup bottle stood upright on the end of a table that was split in half. "It's a miracle," she said, pointing at the site. "No one was eatin' in section 4."

I walked across the aisle to the bar and ordered a Bushmills. The bar was oval-shaped. A hockey game between the Bruins and Sabers, to which no one seemed to be paying any attention, was playing on a television bolted to the wall above the register. The woman beside me was making circles on the bar top with an empty box of Virginia Slims.

She saw me watching and said, "It was a tough choice: gin or the fags. I figured I needed the drink more."

My stomach squirmed a little when she said "fags." She had a British accent. I smiled, trying, though, to be disengaged.

The rule of distance. The columnist's M.O.: Don't get too close unless you can use what's coming at you.

I wanted my drink.

I noticed a man across the bar was watching me. He averted his eyes when he saw me look at him. His thick black hair was flecked with gray. He wore a charcoal herringbone jacket with a blue denim shirt and a dark blue tie. He watched the bartender swipe a credit card through a machine and glanced at the hockey game and then back at me, averting his eyes again when he saw me still looking. He turned back to see if I'd looked away. I hadn't.

It usually started this way: *He's handsome*, I thought. My way of escaping everything.

He fixed his attention squarely ahead, his brow furrowed slightly to let me know he'd decided to study me too. He sipped his drink without looking away. He had a thick 5-o'clock shadow, and when he lifted his arm to drink, I noticed a gold band on his left hand.

I thought about the AZT inside the firefighter's medicine cabinet. Sarah and Jamie were waiting in Providence, but still I watched him. I felt a narcotic slide toward a precipice where decency and good sense ended. When he tipped his glass in my direction, I picked up mine and smiled. He didn't look away—a compatriot in fear and longing.

I decided to approach him, but he left his seat and turned around the curve of the bar. He was wearing stone-washed jeans and walked with an expectation I'd recognized before in other men. He stopped and patted my back and said, "I'm Michael."

The woman beside me stopped twirling her box of Virginia Slims and watched him as he walked away.

"Some guys have all the luck," she said, and left.

Michael watched me from across the corridor, and when he was certain my eyes were shadowing him, he entered the men's room. I found him at the end of a long row of urinals. He stared straight ahead except for the one quick look he shot me when I walked in.

I stood by a sink near the door and waited for the man pissing beside him to leave. I stepped to the urinal and saw him looking down at my crotch. I unzipped and pulled out my cock. He fingered his back into his fly, but still hadn't looked at me. I thought, *This game is over. Thank God.*

Then he nodded and cracked a nervous smile. He turned and walked into a stall. When he left, the flush triggered by the electronic eye startled me. I heard the door to the stall close, but not the sound of the latch. I felt almost as if I was someone else doing this and was surprised that the more furtive my actions became, the more compelling was my desire. I understood that he'd entered the stall to begin a risky milk run. He probably had a wife and children back home, and they didn't matter. Through the slit one of his eyes kept watch to see if I'd be drawn as far. He sat on the toilet seat and tapped a foot, signaling, *hurry up.*

Hand dryers clicked on and blew out hot air. Stall doors opened and shut. Someone passing by said to a friend, "Fucking Knicks deserve to tank."

I could see his shoes flat on the floor, his socks and the bottom of his jeans. I paused long enough to understand it didn't matter that others might be watching. I was lost to what I was doing. I stepped to the stall and opened the door just wide enough to slip in. I pulled it shut and latched it. Michael appeared to be a mirror of my obsession when he looked up. He didn't say a word. His belt and pants were undone. He took a scrap of toilet paper, wetted it with his tongue and stuck it against the red electronic eye above the toilet. He leaned back and lifted his ass far enough to pull down his briefs and jeans to his knees.

I let him be the aggressor. He undid my belt and pants

buckle, unzipped my fly. My pants fell. My erection stuck out of the slit in my boxers. He leaned forward and touched the tip of it with his tongue. He pulled the boxers down and sucked me silently until I came. When I pulled up my shorts and pants, he looked at me. He was satisfied, sorry, and humiliated. I didn't want to suck his cock, and he didn't care. He leaned back again, and I turned and left.

On the way out I kicked something across the floor. It was a prescription bottle of pills and a Bart Simpson chess piece tied together with string.

Jesus, I thought, and looked around the room, expecting to see Stephen Hart somewhere.

I reached under the sink where they'd skidded and fetched them. The pills were the AZT from the bathroom cabinet. Michael had come out of the stall and gave me a look. I put them in my pocket and didn't say anything to him.

Back at the departure gate for my flight to Providence, the last few passengers were waiting to board. I wondered what in the world was happening. I looked around again and thought, *He's here.*

"We need to see some picture I.D., sir," an agent said.

I fished out my wallet and removed my driver's license. A card fell to the floor: THE SLAUGHTER—A DEN AWAY FROM HOME. The young man picked it up and handed it to me.

"Thanks," I said, showing him the license.

He looked at the picture and said, "Great."

My seat was in the window bulkhead exit row. The seat next to me was empty. I stood in the aisle and looked down it to see if he'd followed me on and wondered, *Why would he do this?*

Nervous, I picked up the plastic emergency instruction

card with red X's marking the exit doors and pictures of men and women flinging hatches open. I sat down and covered my face with my hands. I closed my eyes looking for the balm that sometimes comes with the dark. Instead, I pictured Sarah and Jamie. I saw the firefighter kneeling naked at his bed. I shifted in my seat, Homer Simpson and the bottle of AZT pressed into my thigh. I thought, *Jesus, what's happening?* I was dizzy, back inside the metal bathroom stall, the smell of defecation in the air, and a stranger sucking me into oblivion.

The emergency instruction card fell to the floor. I opened my eyes and looked down at the card and wanted to step from the open hole in the plane right into the sky.

■

Lights were lit strategically for me when I arrived home. First, I checked on Jamie, who was asleep with the end of her pillow tucked under her chin. The comforter rose and fell slightly when she breathed. Watching her made me feel worthless.

I walked to the bathroom down the hall, not to the one off the bedroom where Sarah was sleeping. I pulled down my pants and poured Cool Mint Listerine into the cup of one hand and spread the stinging antiseptic over my genitals, and thought, *Right, like this is going to help?*

At the bedroom doorway I checked on Sarah. She stirred. "You're home. A long trip."

I sat on the edge of the bed and drew my hand across her cheek.

"I'll tell you about it in the morning," I said.

"You work too hard," she said, still half asleep.

"I'm going down to write Sunday's column," I said, not

sure she'd heard me before she went back to sleep. Her
ability to give herself so effortlessly to the night amazed
me. She believed it was because she didn't worry. No
demons. And soon I was going to toss her contentment out
the window.

"Sarah," I whispered.

She didn't answer.

Downstairs, I poured myself another whiskey—neat—
and took it and the bottle to my study. Dimmed track lighting cast a kind of twilight on the bookcases behind my
desk. On the shelves were a few family photos. In one, my
daughter wore a skeleton mask and had knife-like finger-
nails. She was six. She curled her fingers and faced me, head
to head, with all of the made-up malevolence she could
muster at her age. I shielded my face with my hands and
opened my mouth.

Next to it was a photo of Sarah and me taken last winter. We were on a footbridge in the Everglades. We were
leaning back on the wooden rail and posing cheek to cheek
before a thick sea-grape tree. Sarah's arm was around my
shoulder and she was about to kiss me. I remembered Jamie
saying, when she took the picture, "OK, guys, look like you
really love each other."

I thought about the Hemingway house in Key West. I'd
gone there alone but it was closed. Scores of cats with six-
toed paws prowled the grounds. On the way back I passed a
private resort, and through an open arch I glimpsed a man
in the pool, kneeling, immersed in the water, sucking another man's cock. The man came up for air and went back
down. Nearby someone sitting in a lounge chair touched his
balls. The night had smelled like sex. All of Key West had
smelled like sex.

The bottle of pills and the Homer chess piece pressed into

my thigh. I put them on the desk and drank some more whiskey.

I thought, *Jesus Christ, he's stalking me. He followed me to the airport, flew to Chicago and he might be here in Providence. He's probably not even a firefighter. What the fuck is going on?*

I drank another whiskey and fingered through a stack of letters from readers that Sarah had picked up from the newsroom. Ideas for Sunday's column.

Someone had written in the small, unsteady script of an elderly person:

> Dear Dan,
>
> My son hasn't called me in 483 days. He lives in Texas, in Houston, and he makes a lot of money in the lottery. He doesn't win the money, he makes the machines the tickets come out of. I know he makes a lot of money because he sends me some of it every month. It comes about the third or the fourth of the month, always without a letter. I save the envelopes because I like to look at his handwriting. It hasn't changed since he went to college. Handwriting isn't like a person. Sometimes I take out all of the envelopes and look at my name he's written (it always looks the same) and wonder if he had a picture of me in his head when he was writing it. Anyway, I hope you write some more about your mother. I know she passed away. But I like the way you remember things about her. Her name was Ann, wasn't it? Mine is Rose. My son's Harry.

In another letter, someone told me he didn't think the homeless guy with the sign—FREE WORK FOR LUNCH—deserved so much ink. He said Ronald Reagan had it right years ago when as president he'd said, "The homeless are homeless because they want to be."

I turned on my computer and watched the blue sky with the winsome clouds of Windows flow onto the screen. I felt drunk and knew I had to file a column tomorrow. I put the bottle of AZT and Homer inside a desk drawer and started to write:

> The homeless guy who holds the sign FREE WORK FOR LUNCH at the Route 95 exit ramp to Atwells Avenue in Providence probably has a mother somewhere who sits in a recliner in a living room full of bric-a-brac and memories until she falls asleep some nights thinking about the son she hasn't heard from in 6,000 days.
>
> When I was a kid, my mother used to love *Queen for a Day*. Later at night, together, we'd watch *The Honeymooners*, and I remembered my mother wincing when Ralph Kramden raised his fist to his wife and said, "To the moon, Alice, to the moon."
>
> At the end of a night when the television goes dark, I feel sorry for the mother of the homeless man who spent the day holding a sign on an exit ramp in Providence. I bet she's thinking about the son who hasn't called and remembers the evening he kissed her on his way to bed when he was her small boy.
>
> My mother lived alone in a house in Lackawanna, New York, before she died. She used to shut off the television and all its noise and call me late at night because she knew I'd be up alone at my desk.
>
> She liked to talk about the weather. It was always too hot or always too cold. Too much snow or too

little sun. Sometimes she talked about health threats and disasters.

Once she called and just said, "Mold."

I recognized her voice from that one word. "What are you talking about, Ma?" I asked her.

"It's in the basements, and it's killing people," she said. "A couple in Erie died yesterday. When it gets into the air, you breathe it in, your throat closes up, you're dead. I saw it on the television news."

She wanted to make sure I tested the basement for mold. That's all she wanted to tell me. She was tired and wanted to sleep.

I miss her now.

Earlier this evening I called home and told my daughter I was stuck in Chicago's O'Hare Airport. She's 17 and ready to leave for college soon. She told me she went to the Stations of the Cross for the first time in her life and decided she prefers Zen. I laughed.

I spoiled everything and told her that things would have been empty without her. I was feeling blue and sorry for myself. I'd never told her anything like this before. Her voice lost its lightness and I regretted sending her off to the night with my burden on her back.

I'm afraid of losing her.

I saved the column even though I knew it wouldn't work. It was sentimental and disorganized. I looked at the pills and thought about getting AIDS and couldn't understand why he would follow me.

I poured some more whiskey and read another letter. It was from a kook named Buddy. He hated most of what happened to him every day. Once he'd written and said he admired my columns and believed that I was the only one in America who got things straight—morally so, like the Boy Scout oath. And forget about women, he'd said, they can't get a fucking thing straight. His letters made me wonder if there was any hope for us at all. He called me Danny Boy, and when he first wrote, he'd said that if I wanted to trade in my eggplant he'd send me a good potato. The Irish, he said, though he didn't want to hurt my feelings, could outsmart a dago any day. It annoyed me that a man like this would like my columns.

This was what he had to say this time.

Dear Danny Boy,

You're right about the parking ticket militia in Providence. Give a schmuck a little authority and you have the foundation for a totalitarian state where fear and suspicion rule. I hate these pawns of government. They're all fags.

Keep the fight alive,
Buddy

All fags, I thought.

I crumpled the letter and threw it in the trash. I clicked onto the Web and did a search for AZT. I clicked on an item called "AZT won't learn to dance":

It's called zidovudine or AZT. It's in the family of nucleoside reverse transcriptase inhibitors. It can delay death when the body breaks down the drug into chemicals that fend off HIV from infecting healthy cells. Cells already infected, though, are out of luck. That's why people who take AZT still die.

These days people take it with two other drugs,

what's called the AIDS cocktail, the triple combination therapy that delays death longer than AZT can
alone. Research proves AZT diminishes dementia.
People forget less and personalities don't change as
drastically. Recently, researchers are understanding
why AZT doesn't work as well as it should. It's just
a bad dance partner. The first time an enzyme
latches on and takes AZT for a spin, the drug kicks
up its heels just fine. The trouble happens when
another enzyme cuts in, and AZT turns up its nose.

A triple combination therapy. A trifecta at Saratoga. A
dance. Hogarth's *Waltz of Skeletons*. I closed the file and
searched for AIDS. There were 1,897,876 items to scroll
through. I chose one called "What AIDS Looks Like." On a
shining black background emerged depictions of cells as
they become infected. The pictures reminded me of bubble-
tipped anemones. I was surprised by how beautiful the disease looked.

I clicked on the transmission tie-in. On a gray screen,
without any fancy graphics, four ways of getting infected
with HIV were listed in order of the highest risk. "Number
one: Penetration in anal or vaginal intercourse where infected fluids are exchanged."

I looked at the bottle of AZT on my desk and felt him
enter me again.

I called up Switchboard USA on the computer and typed
in *Stephen Hart, Seattle, WA*, and almost instantly his name,
address and phone number appeared. It was midnight on
the West Coast. I punched in his number on the phone, and
it rang only once before someone answered:

"Detective Enger," he said.

"The police…" I said, fumbling for a response.

"Do you know Mr. Hart?" he asked.

"An acquaintance," I said.

"It's late for an acquaintance to be calling," he said.

I hung up.

Jesus, I thought, *I shouldn't have hung up. They can easily trace me. Why are the cops in his apartment?*

I clicked on RealPlayer and found a television station in Seattle that replayed the 11 o'clock news on its Web site.

A reporter was standing outside Stephen's apartment house overlooking Volunteer Park. She was standing in the glare of klieg lights and holding a microphone and paging through notes. Her hair was blowing, and her voice was slightly out of sync. She said the police found the firefighter in his apartment after being called by a neighbor. The police weren't releasing any more details. Then the anchor thanked her and said the weather would be coming up.

It was past 3 in the morning and I poured another whiskey and then another. He wasn't stalking me. He was dead. In the morning I'd call the Seattle cops. I'd give them the bottle of AZT and Homer. I thought about Sam and Stephen's broken rib. I'd tell the police everything I knew. I didn't want to call them now because I'd been drinking and there was too much to think about first. Tomorrow, I'd tell them everything I knew. I'd talk to Sarah and Jamie. Nothing would be the same.

I turned off all the lights and sat back down at my desk. I could see the moon like a scythe and a few bright stars through the narrow windows where the ceiling met my bookshelves. My breaths were labored and scared me.

Stephen Hart had been murdered, and I was being drawn into it. I'd have to tell Sarah everything: *A firefighter fucked me. And by the way, he probably had AIDS. And guess what? He was murdered the day after we fucked. Someone is stalking me.*

But the secret itself, the big lie I'd been living for years, would be all she'd need to hate me. And Jamie. What had I done to her?

I was drunk and decided to go upstairs. I took off my clothes and climbed into bed. I felt the heat from Sarah's body crossing the narrow chasm in our bed where sleep, hollow and solitary, had always, sooner or later, found me, too.

purgatory chasm

I heard them in the kitchen. "Go wake your father," my wife said.

My daughter's footsteps on the stairs were light and energetic.

She appeared in the doorway. "Hey, Dad. It's 9 o'clock. Let's get movin'."

"I'm up," I said.

"How was Seattle? Did you know grunge started there?" She was leaning in the doorway.

"All I saw was the inside of conference rooms."

"Next time I want to go with you. I'm tired of Providence. But it better not be a place like Detroit." She squinted, a kind of mock envy, pretending that I owed her some attention.

"Detroit has Aretha Franklin," I said. "Motown, the Temptations, and Smokey Robinson and the Miracles."

She came over and sat on the side of the bed. "They don't live there," she said.

Then she started to sing part of "Cloud Nine," pretending to be one of the Temptations: 'My father didn't know the meaning of work. He disrespected Mama and treated us like dirt.'"

"That's cruel. When did I ever treat you like dirt?"

"It's a song, Dad. What's wrong with you?"

"A mood," I said, waving my hand across my face to help her believe nothing was really wrong.

"I have an idea. Aidan and I are taking Johnny to the 'Bare Bones' exhibit. Do you want to go?"

"You're asking your father to tag along on a date with your boyfriend?"

She was enjoying herself again. "It's not a date. We're taking his little brother to the zoo. Besides, Aidan likes you. I don't know why."

She was fascinated with the "Bare Bones" exhibit at the Roger Williams Zoo: 40 animals, life-size, reassembled from dried bones of carcasses found on the sides of highways, roadkill—coyote, frog, deer, skunk, dog—the skeletal pieces bleached ghostly white. She said she wanted to study paleontology and dig up bones all over the world. Her dream was to discover a wooly mammoth in the Siberian ice cap.

"I'll go," I said.

"Great." She shot me a girlish smile and, humming something I didn't recognize, she went downstairs.

It almost seemed that nothing had changed until I remembered Stephen Hart being wheeled out on a gurney, the pills in my desk drawer, and the notion of a killer stalking me.

I thought, *First, I have to call the Seattle police, talk to the detective…Enger…who answered the phone last night, then I'll contact the cops here. I'll call Jared. I'd have to tell Sarah.* The prospect of explaining this left me breathless. And when I showered, everything rushed back in: The yearlong incubation period for HIV. It could be that long before the disease showed up in a blood test. How Stephen tucked his head against my chest—the satisfying rhythm of his breathing. And now he was dead inside the Seattle morgue.

I considered Stephen's old lover Sam: Was he the killer shadowing me? A reporter, maybe with *The Seattle Times,* maybe a newspaper nearby. I'd check it out. Maybe he was at the conference. I'd tell Enger. Maybe he heard my lecture. The cops would learn where he'd been since the murder and if he'd been seen at O'Hare. The delay from storms moving east of Chicago left him time to track me down. *Jesus,* I thought, *if he didn't leave the pills and Homer outside the stall, who did?* I pictured the old nipple-clamp guy at the Slaughter, his look when Stephen came back with my whiskey. *Surely, it had to be someone he knew, not just random, not someone shunned in the dark bar. Not the nipple-clamp guy.*

I turned up the hot water and let it strike my chest. I wanted to be sorry for the firefighter but instead I thought about how unlucky I was. I'd wanted to stay the night and know the company of a man that wasn't only quick and dirty. I envisioned his corpse, in bed or on the couch next to the chess game. Had he been shot? Suffocated with the same black-and-white checkered pillow I'd slept on? Sam could have followed us home from the Slaughter and waited outside until I left and summoned Stephen back to the apartment.

Jesus—the pills. Whose name was on the bottle of pills? Maybe they were Sam's. Was I this stupid? I'd never looked.

I'd find out when I got downstairs. Maybe Stephen didn't have AIDS. After all, he'd told me he was negative. How could he lie about this? His note that I took back to bed: "Fucking beautiful." He said Sam wasn't gentle. I pictured a fireplace log coming down on him, crushing his skull. How could any of this have happened?

I turned, and my arm knocked the shampoo from the shower shelf. When I bent down to pick it up, my legs wanted to give way. I sat in the tub, the shower spray, striking me hard in the face.

■

When I walked into the kitchen, Sarah was working on the *Times* crossword.

She got up and poured me a cup of coffee. She kissed me on my ear. "I missed you," she said.

"Likewise," I said. She likes the phrase. Sometimes I think she likes it better than *I love you*.

"What's the word for whatever happens next to last?" she asked.

"Penultimate," I said.

"That's it. I've got this one licked. How was Seattle?"

"Tiring. I never picked up the Dungeness crab."

"Figures. What's an eight-letter word for something with a stinging bite that begins with 'a' and ends with 'd'?"

There was silence for about a half minute. We were both thinking words. Nothing clicked.

"I've got something to tell you," I said, in a low voice, but loud enough for her to hear if she were really listening. She wasn't.

Before that morning, after I'd had an *encounter* with a man, it always amazed me how easy it was to talk, as if there had been no betrayal. After all, an *encounter* was something I couldn't help. And she made it easier because she wasn't suspicious. She didn't check my pockets for credit card receipts, didn't quiz me about being out late, assuming I was working hard or drinking hard with other hard-drinking reporters. Sometimes I blamed her: *If only you didn't make this so goddamn easy, the truth would have come out long ago.* I was *that* selfish. But the firefighter wasn't just another encounter. Even if he hadn't been killed and someone hadn't followed me, the morning would have been different from all others. But she wasn't listening.

"Jamie's asked me to go to the zoo too," she said.

She talked without raising her head from the puzzle. I thought, *I'll just start by saying, "Sarah, I'm gay."*

"Sarah," I said.

"Wait, I just want to get this row. I need to concentrate for a few minutes."

I remembered the pills in the desk and decided to check them out. I'd give her some time. She wasn't ready for this seismic shift. I thought, *Maybe it would be better to think everything through first.*

On the way to my study, through a narrow window along the door frame, I noticed a box on the porch. The label was white with blue waves, the kind of ice-packed box used to deliver lobsters. Chelsea, the Lab–border collie mix from next door, was sniffing at it aggressively. I tapped the window and she backed away. She barked at the box and then ran off.

"That dog sounds like it's barking on our doorstep," Sarah called after me.

"It's Chelsea."

"What's slang for oblivion and begins with 'p-a'?" She was still in the kitchen.

I didn't answer. "Never mind," she said, "it's Palookaville."

Marked on the side of the box was PIKE'S MARKET in bright-red letters. I hadn't gone near Pike's Market.

I opened the door. A damp spring draft blew in.

"Are you going outside?" she asked.

"Checking for mail."

"You know the mail doesn't come before 2."

"Must be the jet lag. Time's all screwed up."

I kept the door open with the back of my foot and looked toward the kitchen to see if she was still seated at the table.

I picked up the box, and whatever was inside slushed around. I took it to my study, placed it on top of the trash can next to my desk, and returned to the kitchen.

"I'm going to try to reach someone on the phone to interview. Give me about an hour to myself," I said.

"Sure," she said. She had finished only about half of the puzzle.

Chelsea was back on the stoop, sniffing the square wet stain that the box had left on the concrete. I opened the door. "Get the hell out of here," I said, waving my hand over her head. She bolted.

"What's wrong?" Sarah asked.

"Stupid dog," I said.

"She should be leashed. Do you know who the Bombers in the Bronx are?"

"The Yankees."

"Right."

I returned to the study and lifted the box onto the blotter on my desk. There was no return address, not even a name. The bottom stamped a rust-colored square on the blotter.

I took the letter opener that Sarah had given me one Christmas—round cherrywood so smooth it felt silken—

and sliced the tape on the folds and opened it. Inside, Styrofoam pellets sloshed in rusty water and melting ice.

I poked through the pellets with the silver blade, but I couldn't see anything in the mush; the churning uncovered a pungent metallic smell and a rank odor—blood and something I couldn't identify. I eased my hand in and felt what must have been part of a fish, without scales, a skinned fillet. But even before I clasped it, I worried it wasn't fish flesh.

I wanted to let go, but my hand froze. I pulled it out and held it, the rust-colored water running down my palm into my shirt sleeve. I was too stunned to drop it right away. It was a penis, and attached to it by a few tiny pins was a typed note, laminated, the size of a Post-it: DEFIANCE ENGINE 5.

It fell back into the box, and water splashed up across my cheeks. *What if Sarah or Jamie walked in now?*

I reached back in for the note:

> Don't think of contacting the cops. Don't tell any-
> one. Follow my orders. First, get rid of this souvenir.
> I'd hate to think what I could do to you and your
> pretty wife and kid. Don't forget to take your morn-
> ing-after pills—and say hi to Homer.

I shut the door to my study, and for the first time that I could recall, I locked it. Outside the window I saw Chelsea sniffing again at the porch stoop.

I stood over the desk and felt sick. *Homer, the pills,* I thought, taking them out of the drawer. The container label: AZT. A patient's name worn off; the date, a prescription years old; the pharmacy's name barely recognizable. Then, remembering the box, I thought, *Jesus, this thing.*

I looked in and realized ice had kept the penis from

shriveling into itself. Floating on top of the pellets it looked large and fleshy still. With the blood drawn out, it had an unearthly hue. The veins along its shaft had collapsed and looked like gristle in raw chicken. Its end was serrated. All at once my whole body trembled. I turned and vomited into the wastebasket.

The phone rang and somebody answered it. I picked up the blotter with the box that held Stephen Hart's dismembered penis and hurriedly put everything on the floor behind my chair.

"It's for you, Dan," Sarah shouted from the kitchen.

I stared at the desktop and heard her footsteps. She tried to open the study door.

"What's wrong?" she said. "Why'd you lock the door?"

I opened it. "I must have inadvertently flipped the lock."

"It's Roger. He said he's got a surprise." She walked closer and retrieved a couple of Styrofoam peanuts from the carpet. I moved the basket under my desk because I was afraid she'd smell the vomit and see everything.

"I hate these things," she said, looking for the trash. "They don't decay for hundreds of years. Where's the basket?"

"Here, I'll take them. The basket's under the desk."

She handed me the pellets.

"What's that smell?"

"A carton of sour milk from last night. I'll dump it out later."

She paused and said, "I forgot. He's been waiting on the phone. What's wrong with you anyway? You're even more spacey than usual."

Then she turned away and said, impatiently, "Talk to Roger. I'm going upstairs to shower."

"Tell Jamie not to disturb me."

She turned back and gave me a look.

I picked up the phone and heard the click when Sarah put down the handset in the kitchen before she went upstairs. I said hello and looked down at the box. I didn't know whether I could keep the phone to my ear.

Roger was *The Record*'s editor in chief. At 70 he was more passionate about newspaper writing than anyone I'd known. I was still one of his great hopes.

He wanted to tell me I'd been nominated for the regional AP award in commentary writing. He talked for about five minutes. He said the judges were struck by how matter-of-factly I showed petty corruption destroying so many city hall workers. "Calamari for a kingdom," he said. "They liked that line." I didn't hear a tenth of what he was telling me.

While he spoke, I stared at the dismembered penis. I think I said I didn't deserve the award, because he then said he'd never heard this kind of modesty from a columnist before. He said he'd hoped we could celebrate later that night. I don't think I said goodbye.

All the while I was thinking, *How am I going to tell the cops, after that note?* I tried again to picture faces, men from the Slaughter, the airport, someone on my plane: the nipple-clamp man, the boy-bartender, the priest calling to the nuns, a few college kids, the trick in the stall. *Jesus*, I thought, *the trick, someone with a ring, married like me. Maybe he's the reporter who beat up Stephen? But what about the pills and Homer outside the stall door? The trick couldn't have placed them there without me noticing? And, Jesus, what about the note ordering me to get rid of this?*

I lifted the box back on the desk. The foul water ran onto the carpet and down my arm again. The penis bobbed in the mushy mess of Styrofoam and melted ice. The plastic bag lining the wastebasket I'd vomited in looked big enough. I pulled it out and dropped every-thing in. I tore April from the blotter, tore out other soiled months up to October, which was dry. I stuffed the calendar pages into the bag. I twirled the bag in circles until there was a strip long enough to tie it shut. I didn't know what I was going to do. But I couldn't call the detective in Seattle until I'd thought everything through. I couldn't tell Sarah until I'd taken this out of the house.

She appeared at the doorway again.

"I thought you were taking a shower," I said.

"I left my robe in the laundry room. What was Roger's surprise?"

"Nothing important."

I leaned on the desk with one hand and covered the AZT so she wouldn't see it.

"He said he had some really good news."

"It wasn't anything."

She shook her head. "You're as communicative as ever," she said, uncharacteristically sarcastic. "What's in the bag?"

"Garbage. Old papers I started clearing out last night." I couldn't believe she didn't notice my distress. She'd grown accustomed to dispelling any suspicion, and I'd learned how to lie almost effortlessly.

"We're supposed to meet Jamie in an hour at the zoo." She left, humming something that sounded like a Ricky Nelson song as she went back upstairs.

I looked at the bag and inspected my hands for small cuts where the water might have entered. I wondered whether infected blood diluted with water and packed in ice could transmit the disease. I'd get a test in 30 days and every few months for a year. Then I'd know. I wanted to feel sorry for Stephen Hart, but there was too much going on.

■

I didn't go to the zoo. I told them that my column was a mess. I'd have to go to the newsroom to do some research and then rewrite it. I lied. Actually, I'd filed a piece, something stock that I'd kept in the can for a time like this, when writing was impossible. The desk editors wouldn't be surprised. They knew me better than Roger or the AP. I think they suspected I was a fraud. Too often I wrote like an uninspired documentary filmmaker who has perfect pitch for showing things as they are, but no reach beneath the surface. I gained the confidences of others. Maybe I satisfied readers and moved them when I dressed up cliches. But I didn't see beneath the surface in their lives, or my own. I didn't see that a catastrophe usually starts like a crack on the sea bottom long before the earth shifts and the massive displacement of water begins. A catastrophe like this when everything familiar was fractured. A dismembered penis in a bag. A maniac shadowing me. A secret life about to explode in the faces of two people I'd loved so carelessly for so long.

I thought, *I've got to find out who Sam is.* It was a little before noon—three hours earlier on the West Coast—and I decided to call a columnist I knew from *The Seattle Times.* His name was Richard Bellemy, and he was famous for slice-of-life pieces, a kind of Charles Kuralt of print journalism. He'd done a series about a gay couple dying of AIDS in a remote town in the Cascades. In the end the two men carried out a suicide pact because neither wanted to be left without the other. Bellemy watched them die. It was before the AIDS cocktail became widely available. He's straight, and the Lambda Literary Foundation gave the work a special award. The series was short-listed for the Pulitzer. He wasn't a fraud.

I think he was surprised to hear from me. We exchanged some chatter about the conference and the nasty storms he'd read about on my return home. Then I asked him whether he could help me out.

I said, "I'm looking for a crime reporter from the area, maybe even on the *Times* staff. His name is Sam. I don't know his last name."

"No Sam on our staff. Where'd you meet him?"

"At the conference. Can you think of anyone nearby?"

"Not off the top of my head, but I can ask around."

"Great, I'd appreciate it."

"Really, your speech on the confidence man was great. You took us off our pedestal. Hey, I read on the AP that you're up for a regional award."

"Yep," I said, looking nervously at the trash bag. "I've got to run. Call me if you come up with anyone. It's important."

"What's this all about, Dan?"

"It's kind of personal."

"Off-the-record then?"

"Right, like anything is off-the-record among columnists. I just need a favor."

"You're making it more intriguing than it probably is."

"It's personal, Rich. Trust me. It's not anything you'd want to know."

"I'll check around for anyone named Sam on a crime beat and call you."

"I'll owe you." And we said goodbye.

I'd heard Sarah and Jamie leave while I was on the phone. I carried the trash bag to my car and put it into the trunk. Chelsea came over and sniffed the blacktop where it had rested while I fumbled for my keys. She snorted at the bare pavement. I started the engine. There were small leaves on the gigantic copper beeches in our front yard.

Patches of tulips had sprung up here and there. I didn't
exactly know what I was going to do with the dismembered
penis in my trunk. I turned to look at the house and then
headed for the ocean.

■

It was just past 1 o'clock when I turned into the gravel
lot at Purgatory Chasm. Mist and thick patches of fog blew
off the water. My senses were heightened, the way the mind
and body reopen after a shock that's left you nearly numb.
The tires crunched across the gravel. The foghorn sounded.
The car breathed, and the click of the ignition when it shut
off was like a hammer releasing on a gun.

There were no other cars in the lot. No one I could see
who was watching. Usually, it was packed with pickups,
vans, Volvos, Jeep Cherokees, rusted Chevrolets and Fords.
You'd see felt dice dangling from a rearview mirror, or
plastic suns and rabbits stuck to a window next to a child-
protector seat, or bumper stickers praising the Lord and
defending gun owners. GO NAVY on a window or bumper
meant a sailor was out cruising. The drivers were men, and
they arrived alone and walked on paths through scrub
leading to the rocky cliff and wooden bridge over the
chasm. Many left the paths, as I'd done a few times, for a
small clearing where others were waiting. No one knew
anyone when he arrived, and no one wanted to know anyone when he left. That afternoon mist hung in the air like
wet gauze.

I was careful to look around before I opened the trunk
and took out the bag. I was certain no one had followed
me. I thought, *Maybe he's finished with me now. Maybe he's
back in Seattle and the worst of it is over.* There was nothing

else remotely cautious about what I'd decided to do. The leafless scrub tore small cuts in the bag as I walked along the path. Bloody water leaked out. When I got to the wooden bridge, I set down the bag. In breaks between thick patches of fog, I saw the frothing water sweep into the chasm and then subside. The chasm sliced out about 100 feet and descended about the same distance from the cliff top to the water. The gap in the rock was only a few feet wide, maybe a little more in places, not enough for a body to dive cleanly through. The limestone was too steep to slide down either side.

For one terrifically clear moment I thought of leaping. I imagined my skull cracking open against the rock, my bones breaking, some ribs, a leg, an elbow, and if I were lucky, my neck snapping before I hit the water. I looked out into the mist to scan as much of the gray Atlantic that was visible, and thought, *Fat chance, I'm not getting out of this so easily.*

I removed the box from the bag, reached my hand in and grabbed hold of Stephen Hart's penis. There was no more ice, not even much water left. I lifted it from the slimy Styrofoam pieces. I didn't hold it for more than a few seconds before tossing it into the chasm. The water was roiling from a storm far out in the Atlantic and there was too much mist to see whether it had hit the water or bounced off the rock. I flipped over the box to dump the Styrofoam, but most of the pieces scattered in the wind behind me onto the path and into the scrub. I let the bag, stinking with my own vomit, blow away too. It snagged on a rose-hip bush. Then I threw the box into the gorge, and through a brief clearing in the fog, I saw it being tossed by the chaos below. In a few weeks, on Earth Day, a troop of Boy Scouts would probably sweep through the scrub as they did every spring and clear away the mess.

The fog thickened again and obscured everything. I hoped Stephen Hart was dead when the murderer cut off his penis. I wasn't angry with him anymore for bringing me home and letting his condom break inside me. I thought, *I should have given the penis and the box to the police; there might have been a way to trace them to the killer. If Sam did this, he might have left some evidence behind. Instead, I've done exactly what he wanted.*

■

I drove down Newport's Bellevue Avenue past the mansions of Astors and Vanderbilts to where the gas-lit street turned into Ocean Drive. Everything along the meandering shore was a shade of gray: the sky, the water, the road, the thick wet air itself. The colorlessness made it all seem like a grainy silent-era film. While I drove through the fog, I felt an unexpected relief: I almost didn't exist.

I pulled in to Brenton Point and parked facing the shore's rocky edge. The foghorn from Jamestown Light reverberated in my chest. A seagull landed on the hood and watched me through the windshield. I tapped the glass and it didn't budge. I looked around and thought he'd be somewhere nearby. Or maybe he didn't follow me because he believed he could count on my compliance. Within seconds, after the scavenger flew off, I started the engine and headed back to Providence. I wasn't going home. Not yet.

■

I drove to the newsroom on Fountain Street. My desk was in the back of the expansive room with a ceiling high enough to suspend a half-scale replica of the America's Cup champion *Courageous*. No walls separated the reporters' stations and editorial pods, but computers and stacks of books rose from desks like cairns staking out clan territories. Beside my desk was a floor-to-ceiling arched window. When the sun began to set over Dunkin' Donuts across the street, an automatic shade descended, making the afternoon glare as passive as the high fluorescent light. The newsroom was the place where events of a day were recorded in all of their unpredictability, and still it seemed a refuge—something artificial, an illusory escape. I walked under the gallery of blown-up front-page photographs on giant poster boards: Ted Williams in a baggy gray dress-suit and Red Sox cap at the opening of the tunnel that bears his name in Boston. An aerial view of the city's restored river, which until recently, had been buried under concrete for a half-century. A Cambodian-American boy, maybe 10 years old, standing, dry-eyed, over the body of his dead brother who had been slain by a gang in Olneyville. A makeshift memorial of flowers and photographs to the dead burned in the Station nightclub conflagration. Behind my desk, a photograph of two priests carrying a life-size statue of the Virgin Mary draped with colored lights, an oversize wooden rosary, and a garland of dollar bills.

It was 3 when I arrived. Except for the police-beat reporter shopping for CDs on the Internet, the room was empty. She waved when I walked past her station. Ricky Martin was crooning from her computer speaker.

I opened the deep bottom desk-drawer and poured some whiskey into a coffee mug. I drank it and poured another, the pint invisible to anyone else, and put the mug on my desk.

I called home.

"It's me," I said.

"We just got back. I'd forgotten how much I hate zoos," Sarah said.

"I'm still working. You OK? Anything funny happen?"

"*Funny?* What's got into you?"

"Any messages? Richard Bellemy from *The Seattle Times* might call. If he does, tell him I'll get back to him soon."

"No one called."

"I'll be home late. Don't wait dinner."

"I'll wait," she said and then hung up.

I thought, *She must know something's terribly wrong. I'll tell her tonight. First I've got to find out what he wants from me.*

I logged onto my PC and typed the password: "Jamie." There were nine unread messages, but nothing from Bellemy. The first a fussy note from a copy editor who thought she was being funny when she asked me whether I knew the difference between *pour* and *pore.* "Saved your ass again," she said, adding :}, computer-speak for *just kidding.* I hated it. Several e-mails about my piece on a fire dispatcher. He was 5 foot 8 and weighed 330 pounds, and he didn't think obesity should keep him from active duty. The e-mails were all from men, none sympathetic to the fat dispatcher, who said that if he couldn't get back to fighting fires, he couldn't work at all, claiming mental anguish and suffering. One was filled with jokes like, "Maybe they could use him as a trampoline to catch a suicide jumper." I hadn't liked the column when I wrote it, and afterward I liked it even less.

And there was this:

> I'll be in touch. Remember, don't go to the cops, don't tell your family. I've got plans for you.

This time he gave a name: "Yours truly, Buddy."

Jesus, I thought, *he isn't Sam. He's the sicko whose been sending me bizarre letters for years: Buddy.*

But Buddy had never e-mailed before; he'd always written letters. He once wrote that he hated computers. Why would he start e-mailing? I had talked about him in my lecture—discussed fans who embarrass columnists and make you wonder whether what you wrote was what a reader read. Buddy's comments, I'd said, made me think I was writing in a funhouse mirror. I thought, *Sam: The bastard was at my lecture, and now he's posing as this wacko from home. He isn't going away.*

I tried to e-mail him back and wrote: "Who the fuck are you? What do you want from me?" Moments after I'd sent it, a message popped up from my mail server: "Undeliverable transmission, check address."

Then Rich Bellemy called.

"Dan," he said. "I found three guys named Sam covering crime beats in a wide radius of Seattle."

I felt unsteady and tried hard not to betray it.

"That's great," I said. "Shoot."

"Sam Winchel at the weekly *Ledger* in Port Townsend, Sam Jarzembeck at the *Sun* in Olympia and Sam Sanchez way down in Aberdeen at the *Daily Times.*"

"You know anything about them? Any married?"

"That's a strange question."

I thought, *I better not get him too interested.*

"The guy told me he was married, wanted to write some out-of-his-beat pieces on marriage," I said.

"Mentoring?"

"Sort of."

I could tell he was suspicious.

"I checked out the obvious. Two were registered at the

conference: Winchel from Port Townsend and Jarzembeck from Olympia."

"That's a help."

"And Winchel rang some bell. So I made a records check. It's not pretty. A couple years ago he was charged with beating his wife. He got probation. No contact for a year. Time passes and he moves back with the broad. Go figure." He paused and said, "So what's up. Is he the guy? Does he want to write a book about being a reformed wife-beater?"

"If he's the guy, he didn't mention anything about beating his wife."

"What did he say?"

"Nice try. I told you it's *personal*. It's not that interesting anyway, trust me."

"Trust the confidence man of opinion journalism?" He laughed.

I thought I'd try to find out if he knew anything about Stephen Hart's murder and asked, "So any big stories out there today?"

"It's Easter weekend. You'd expect everything to be pretty low-key, right? Turns out a gay firefighter's been whacked. Gruesome, too. Stiff was cut into pieces. Gays are talking like the killer might be a serial. No leads. It happened Friday morning just after 10. Good Friday. Go figure."

I pictured his cock in my hand. I thought, *Maybe I should tell Bellemy everything. He's a decent man. He could help.*

Instead I said, "Fuckin' psychos, they never stop."

He'd said that Stephen was killed just after 10—less than an hour after I'd left the apartment. *Jesus,* I thought, *was he going back to see me?*

"These guys keep us in business," he said.

"I owe you."

"Why not just tell me what's up."

"I said it's personal."

"What isn't personal with a columnist."

I was wasting time and said, "Got to go. My wife, she wants me home soon."

Before I hung up he said he'd be in touch.

I drank more whiskey and pictured a shadowy figure waiting for Stephen to return to the apartment. I thought: *Was he outside when I left the house? Was he watching the night before from the woods that led to Volunteer Park? Did he have binoculars and see his ex-lover put a hand on my bare ass?* I left this message for the three reporters named Sam at their newspapers: "I know who you are." Then I felt stupid, remembering the even stupider line from a bad movie: "I know who you are and saw what you did." I called up Switchboard USA and looked for their home numbers. Only Sanchez in Aberdeen was listed—the long shot. I left a message there, too. This time I just said, "Call me." But Winchel was the obvious one. He would have gone back to his wife about the time he stopped seeing Stephen Hart. It made sense.

I clicked on *The Seattle Times* digital newspaper. The murder led the page, updated just an hour before. Under the headline FIREFIGHTER DEAD IN VICIOUS ATTACK there was a photograph of the blue and pink Victorian house and a circle of cops and rescue workers wheeling the gurney with a covered corpse.

SEATTLE—A firefighter was murdered in a gruesome killing at his home in the Capitol Hill section of the city Friday morning.

Fire Lt. Stephen B. Hart, 39, of Red Maple Street, was killed, his body mutilated, about two hours after he'd received a call and left Defiance

Engine 5 on Union Street, according to police Detective Anthony Enger. His body wasn't discovered until late that night.

Enger said that Hart's body was naked; parts, which the police would not identify, had been cut off. He said condoms were fastened with safety pins to his chest.

The officers were summoned to the scene after an elderly woman who lives in the apartment below called 911 and reported blood coming from a hole in the ceiling around a steam pipe.

The police have learned that on Thursday night Hart may have gone home with an unknown man whom he met earlier at the Slaughter, a gay dance club near the Space Needle. Witnesses remember Hart leaving about 11:30 P.M., and one witness reportedly saw him and a man in the driveway of Hart's residence at about 11:45.

Enger said the man with Hart at the gay club on Thursday night is being sought for questioning.

I pictured the murder scene. None of it seemed possible. I envisioned the body parts in his apartment and remembered lifting his penis out of the box. I thought, *They're looking for me. Someone saw me outside the house. Would the witness recognize me? Or did he just see a figure in the dark? If someone had been able to identify me, the cops would have released a detailed description. For Christ's sake, why did I hang up on the detective?*

I read the rest of the story.

According to Fire Sgt. Adam Westicoff, Hart left the station after getting a call and had said that there was some problem at home and that he'd try to be back a little after noon.

"He didn't seem too worried," Westicoff said. "He knew whoever called. No one can believe what happened. It doesn't make sense."

The firefighter lived alone in his apartment overlooking Volunteer Park. While the police have no evidence that the killing was a hate crime, its gruesome nature raises the suspicion, said Andrew Wyatt, of the Seattle Gay Human Rights League.

"The gay community is scared," he said.

The police said that they are interviewing witnesses and ask anyone who saw Hart or the man he left the Slaughter with Thursday night to contact them.

I thought, *Someone summoned him. He wasn't going home to me. Jesus, they really think I killed him.*

I panicked. Melanie left Ricky Martin and came over.

"Dan, are you OK?" she asked.

I covered my face in my hands for a few moments until I could collect myself.

"It's an asthma attack," I said. "Fuck the springtime." I smiled and swallowed air.

"Can I help?" She still had her earphones on. The cord dangled down her shoulder and brushed my neck.

"Nothing. Thanks. Sorry I gave you a scare." I must have looked shaky because she didn't want to leave.

"Hey, you're the first emergency I've had in three Saturdays," she said.

I hoped she hadn't seen the story on my computer screen. If she had, she didn't seem interested.

"I'm fine now. The doctor calls it a sudden-impact episode. I'm no worse for wear."

"Hey, you need me for anything, just signal," she said, turning to go back to her terminal.

I made a printout and clicked off the Internet. I drank some more whiskey and decided to call Jared. He'd been investigating gay bashings in the city. I had to find out what he knew without raising suspicions about me. I thought, *Maybe the killer isn't from Seattle. Maybe he's here in Providence.*

About six months ago, a priest was found next to railroad tracks near the Amtrak station, a cruising spot for closeted men. He was naked and had been beaten with a tire iron. When he recovered, the bishop sent him to an order house in Albuquerque, the same place the church sends pedophiles. Jared never found his assailant. He wanted me to talk to the priest and tell the guy's story as a warning to other johns. He told me he thought the priest was getting a raw deal.

"You could do a lot of good," he'd said.

Instead, I asked Mary Jenkins, the *Record*'s other columnist, whether she was interested. I never gave Jared a reason. I didn't explain that telling the priest's story would be an unbearable hypocrisy. I didn't have to. He knew. I passed it on, and ever since I think I've been a major disappointment.

I called the police station.

"I'm looking for Jared O'Connor."

The dispatcher recognized my voice.

"The mighty columnist. Don't you guys ever let up. Hold on. He just walked in," she said.

"Hey, Caruso, why the fuck have you become a stranger all of a sudden?" He could have mentioned the priest and rubbed my conscience in it, but he didn't.

"A little distance from the cops for a journalist isn't so bad once in a while. Look, I'd like to see you. What about a drink?"

"When?"

"Now? Fifteen minutes at Murphy's."

"Fifteen minutes. I've wanted to see you anyway. But you better have something to tell me. This works both ways." He hung up.

He'd started on the force a year before I arrived in Providence. We'd worked the same night beat down-city. At 2 in the morning, just after the final edition was put to bed and everyone else except me and a roving security guard had left the building, I sat at my desk and listened to the police scanner. Sometimes I played solitaire; more often I read crime novels, classics like *The Postman Always Rings Twice*, *The Maltese Falcon*, and *Farewell, My Lovely*.

On a weeknight, the rundown city, years before anyone imagined a Providence renaissance, was a haven for vagrants and petty hoods. There was lots of troublemaking: a smashed window at a liquor store on Washington Street, a woman screaming at a companion in Kennedy Plaza, someone on Federal Hill looking for open doors of parked cars. Petty thieves, dealers, hookers, addicts, and drunks. I'd join him sometimes when I saw him on foot patrol or noticed his cruiser across the street near Haven Brothers. At night, the diner on wheels was parked outside City Hall, the squat circa-1900 building with two round windows like bulging eyes peering down from its mansard roof. If the weather were foul, we'd sit in his cruiser and talk about the city. We were both 25 years old. He was married then, too, smart, and he liked Martin Scorsese movies. Providence wasn't even a wannabe *Mean Streets*, he said to me. New York's the place for action. I agreed, and we gave each other the bored look two good guys share that means without saying it: *life sucks.*

One night we drove to a burned-out mill in the north end. He didn't have to tell me why he'd turned into the lot because I could see what he'd wanted. He'd let his hand brush against my thigh so that it seemed aimless at first but then he cupped it against the inside and started to breathe nervously. I didn't say anything, and he understood my silence was more than surprise, more even than acquiescence. I looked at him and nodded. He parked behind a smokestack in the back of the building, far from the road, where no one could possibly see. I distinctly remember the sound of his fly opening, the way he lifted his ass to slide his pants down to his calves. It was pitch dark. We didn't kiss. But he touched my cheek with his hand tenderly before he guided me into his lap. Believe it or not, he was the first man I'd ever tasted. When it was over, we didn't say anything until he dropped me at the front of the *Record.*

"That won't happen again," he said.

"OK."

"It was kind of an experiment."

"Right."

"And it was OK, but it's over. Pussy's better, right?"

"Right," I said.

I left and walked into the *Record.* That was almost 20 years ago. We'd never mentioned it again.

He was the first man I wanted to love even before that night outside the mill. Sometimes I played a little game to which he was oblivious. If we were in a line at Haven Brothers, I pretended our hands brushed against each other. I imagined saying, *You know, I really like you.* Sometimes at night I dreamed about him naked, and there was nothing sleazy about it. We were two buddies like the Army recruits in my father's Texas photograph.

Back then, on a night when something seriously bad happened, I'd be outside the crime scene, sometimes a murder, more often a break-in or shooting. O'Connor would wave me over, and say, "Here's what I can give you," and I would leave for the newsroom with a real story. I was a witness to a world that, every once in a while, showed me its savage, sexy, and desperate underside. Especially on a night like that, I'd think everything about him was sexy. I'd think, *If a guy like that would want me, I'd have a crack at happiness.* Not long after, I went down on a guy in a bathroom stall. It was nothing like what I really wanted.

■

At Murphy's we sat at a corner table in the back. The tavern was empty except for four men and a woman at the bar, who were drinking pints and watching Keno numbers pop onto state lottery screens at each end of the bar. Sports pennants, photos of city celebrities and framed *Record* front pages covered the pine-paneled walls. Next to our table was the front page from the day after the most destructive hurricane in New England history. The headline: CITY SUNK; HUNDREDS DEAD. Below it, photographs of submerged traffic lights, houses ripped from foundations, boats split into pieces. The stories didn't begin until page 2.

"Cheery spot," Jared said. "Why didn't you pick the mayor's corner?"

He was referring to the table next to a poster of the city's long-time mayor, a convicted criminal now in a federal prison in New Jersey. In the picture he's sitting at his desk with a jar of his own spicy tomato sauce before him and the American flag drooping on a stand in the background.

People called him Ralphie because he looked a little like Jackie Gleason. Jared liked him.

I nodded. "Thanks for seeing me on short notice like this."

"What's a friend for?"

"Right."

I ordered a double Paddy's and he asked for a Bud.

"A double. Must be something serious on your mind."

"The only place in the state with Paddy's. It's important to seize the opportunity."

"Right," he said sarcastically. "You know I never understood why a *covone* like you takes to Irish whiskey. You see me drinkin' chianti?"

"I like to cast a wider net."

"Playing the intellectual is more like it. You writers are all the same. Nose up your ass like everyone else but you don't know it."

I laughed, surprised that I could, without forcing it.

The bartender put down the drinks. Jared lifted his pint and said, "Long live James Joyce."

I didn't say anything.

"What's so important?" he asked.

"I was thinking about those days on the night shift."

"Jesus, what is this, a walk down penny lane?"

"It's memory lane."

"You think I don't know that. Something's up here."

"I want to apologize about the priest."

"Six months go by and you want to apologize. You could have done some good. That piece by Mary Jenkins sucked. How can a broad write about a closeted fag?"

I understood the accusation and didn't go there, even though I knew he hoped I would. I wanted to talk about the night outside the mill. I wanted to tell him about the dead firefighter and everything that happened since I'd awakened alone in his bed. I wanted Jared to embrace me and say, "Don't worry, I'll help you." I thought, *If he'd only loved me years ago, who knows what might have happened?* In the silence he'd left me in, I couldn't tell whether he was waiting me out because he thought I had something important to tell him or whether he was nervous, too.

But I needed information. I wanted to know whether he'd heard anything about gay homicides anywhere. Some common M.O. Condoms pinned to a stiff's chest. *Jesus,* I thought. *Anything about me?*

"Remember the time we were walking your beat and found the foot," I said.

"I was shining my light into doorways and you stopped about halfway through the alley and said, 'Ah, fuck.'"

"That's when I found it next to the Dumpster," I said.

"Freakin' foot of some poor bastard just lying there. Sometimes the old-timers still razz me about it. They tell rookies nobody ever took foot patrol as seriously as I did."

I pictured the firefighter's mutilated body and said, "One of the unsolved mysteries of Providence."

"I think the rest of the guy was mu shu pork all week long," he said.

"I've been considering writing a novel about it," I said and wondered, *Where am I going here?*

He gave me a look: *You're kidding, right?*

I continued: "Like the foot was sent to someone as a warning and that someone knew the guy where the foot came from, identified it somehow. Say that someone, instead of going to the cops, threw the foot away because he was scared and didn't want any more trouble. Say it was some bastard who took the souvenir and sent it off to terrorize this someone. What kind of trouble would the guy be in for tossing the foot?"

It was ridiculous.

"Destroying evidence," Jared said. He was bored. "Probably wouldn't make a difference if the guy really didn't have anything to do with the killing. But a novel about a severed foot sounds like a bad idea."

"I guess."

"Look, I don't mind helping you with fiction, but if that's what you wanted to see me about, let's put it on hold. I've got something serious to discuss."

"The priest?"

"No, you." He looked right at me. *He knows.*

The bartender came over with another whiskey and beer. I drank half of it at once and didn't say anything. Jared waited for the bartender to leave before he continued.

"So let's go down memory lane some more. We've never mentioned that night at the mill," he said.

"I know," I said, astonished that he'd bring it up now.

"For a while, after I divorced Shirley, I thought that maybe I was gay, at least bisexual. Sometimes I thought about guys, sometimes about you, but I didn't feel like doing anything about it. Lots of girlfriends since Shirley, too. Good sex. I guess I grew out of it."

"It?"

"Thinking about guys." He wasn't embarrassed. He'd thought this through and sounded convinced he'd settled the issue. I didn't respond.

"And what about you?" he asked.

"It's not that simple."

"I know. I've seen you in cruising places. Two months ago, I was working in the park across from the train station. You were walking along the river at 2 in the morning. Some kid stopped you, but you turned him down. Good thing, too, because he was 16 and had a knife. Not long after that, I saw you parked outside the Yukon. You waited until the bar closed, talked to a biker who'd just walked out of the dive, and drove away."

I thought about saying I was working a story, some other lie: I 'd been researching gay cruising in the city. Anything. *Like he'd believe me.*

I said, "I'm sorry."

"Fuck sorry. I don't give a shit about your sex life, but I don't want you to end up like the priest, or worse. You heard about the kid's murder, right?

"What murder?"

"Ligget and Borrowski didn't say anything? They're working on the story."

"Not about any murder. When did it happen? I was at a conference most of the week. I haven't talked to any reporters."

"Last week, a Cambodian kid was found tied to a piling in the harbor. He was slashed in about 30 places. Turns out he'd been picking up men by the railroad tracks for months. But nobody knows about that part of it yet."

"Why not?"

"We think there might be a potential serial, we're not sure, but we don't want him to know we're onto him."

"Jesus," I said.

"A sick fuck. So watch your back. No more cruising."

I thought, *If he'd known about the firefighter in Seattle, he'd have said something. Jesus, a serial here. This can't be coincidence.*

I finished my Paddy's and gestured to the bartender.

"That's number three in about a half hour," Jared said. "But who's counting?"

"I think I'd hoped you'd see me," I said. "At the railroad tracks, outside the bar."

It was the kind of thing I thought he'd want to hear. He

didn't say anything. I felt the old attraction mowing me down. I remembered the way he touched my cheek years ago and thought, *Why couldn't he still be interested? Men don't just decide they're straight. He's not married now. Maybe he's hiding from himself—maybe he's as much a coward as me.*

"I'm scared," I said. Then I remembered the note and froze. Buddy had told me not to talk to the cops. What if he'd followed me?

"Scared's OK, for a while. You look like you want to tell me something else."

He paused and left me in another uncomfortable silence. His beeper sounded. "Shit," he said. "I've got to go back to the station. I want to talk again. I don't want to leave it like this. I want to help."

"Help?"

"Yeah, support. You look like you need someone to talk to. You've got a lot to figure out. I figure you can use me as a sounding board. You know, a buddy. Tomorrow's Easter. I'll call you Monday. We'll come back here when I've got more time. You OK tonight?"

"I'm OK."

"Then why do you look like a guy walking out of a burning house?" He patted me on the shoulder and wanted to say something else, but decided not to. He turned and left.

I drank the rest of my whiskey and the beer he'd left and ordered another Paddy's and felt the old compulsion stirring. I should have tried to figure out what to do. There was the dead firefighter. The note from the killer. Purgatory Chasm. I should have let all this worry send me home. I should have told Jared everything. Instead, I invited the booze to lead me on another hunt.

It was 5 when I left Murphy's. The fog and mist had lifted, and the unexpected afternoon sunlight ignited the tan and red bricks of the old Union Station across the street. My head ached. In this bright and extinguishing light there was almost no place to hide.

the berths

On my way to the Weybosset Street Baths, I stopped outside the Travelers Aid building on Washington and watched homeless men set up cots for the night. I didn't want to think about the danger I'd put everyone in. I slipped into Molley's for one more whiskey, and at the bar I envisioned naked and anonymous men next door in the steam. I thought, *None of them wants to be alone.*

The bathhouse was above a shop that sold cigarettes, candy, sodas, and soft-core porn. Its stairwell was painted blackish red, the color of clotted blood, and lit by zigzag red neon that cast shadows like bat wings.

I waited behind a young man in the elevator-size reception room. He slipped a 20 through a slot to the clerk, who then slid open the glass partition and handed him a cheap white towel and buzzed him in. He didn't look much older than a teenager. A Spiderman tattoo covered his arm from the wrist to the cuff of his white T-shirt. Small black letters on his hand spelled out CARNAGE. In a James Dean pose, he draped a leather jacket over his shoulder.

The clerk laughed when I moved up to the window. "Shopping already," he said.

I raised my eyebrows.

"Be careful of that one," he said. "He's advertising. Your membership card, honey."

"I don't have one."

"It's members only. Usually you need a sponsor."

"Usually?"

"Maybe you can convince me you're not nuts, or a cop."

"I'm a minister," I said.

"I'm not impressed. I'm a Jew; a rabbi doesn't impress me. But fine."

Apparently the club's rules were this easy to bend.

He explained that membership cost a hundred bucks. Each visit was another 20. A member had privileges at any of the branches in other cities, including Baltimore, Tampa, Austin, and San Diego. The Weybosset was the only club in New England. He said I'd get a locker and could stay up to 12 hours. There was a steam room, sauna, Jacuzzi, showers, a TV lounge with soft drink machines and free coffee, a smoking area, and about 50 private berths with doors but no locks. He'd have to see a driver's license and keep the number for his records.

I hesitated. I wondered whether he'd recognized me from my column or appearances on local talk shows.

"Credit card?" I said.

"You bet, Father." He knew I wasn't a clergyman.

I gave him my VISA card and looked for my license. "Does the club respect confidentiality?"

"You bet, Father. Only friends of Dorothy here. No snitches. Just make sure you keep your cash and watch locked up tight. No snitches doesn't mean no hustlers. See this?"

He pointed to a sign at the top corner of the glass partition: THE SPA ISN'T RESPONSIBLE FOR LOST OR STOLEN PROPERTY. BE SMART, BE GOOD, PLAY SAFE.

He returned my card and license with a printout receipt to sign. He had huge rings on all of his fingers: one with a turquoise stone, another with a black opal, a gold ring with the carved head of a lion that had two embedded diamonds for eyes. His wrist was wound with silver bands like the end of a lightbulb. In the left side of his nose, a little stone that looked like a sapphire. When I gave him the signed receipt, he noticed my wedding band. *Pathetic*, he probably thought.

"OK, Father. Pony up 20 and I'll send you down the yellow brick road."

"You didn't put it on the Visa?"

"We like cash for the daily visits." He was getting bored.

I slid the bill through the slot at the bottom of the window. He opened the partition with one of his Liberace hands and gave me my membership card, a towel, and a combination for a locker.

"Ready, set, buzz," he said, unlocking the door to the bathhouse rooms.

I put the membership card in my jacket pocket and walked inside. The faint smell of steam mixed with stale, stagnant air. There were round tables and plastic white chairs scattered throughout the room. The carpet was the color of Colorado clay and stained from shoes, spilled coffee and sodas, flattened gum worn into the carpet. Along one wall was a row of pinball machines: Born To Be Wild ("Nothing moves like a Harley Davidson"), Johnny Mnemonic ("the ultimate mind game"), Catacombs ("a chilling game of skill"), and Congo ("hippos, snakes, and killer apes"). A Coke machine lit up a back corner, and across from it was the back of the reception clerk's office, not much bigger than a walk-in closet, with three small round windows. Once in a while I saw the clerk's head bob into view. The door to the office made a nearly seamless fit and across it was a sign: PRIVATE. A phone allowed guests to talk to the clerk, though the offer of a conversation was as inviting as a roadside call box. The long front windows overlooking Weybosset Street were painted black, but from close up, scratches in the glass allowed sightings on the street: a parked car, a cop on a horse, a piece of the flashing marquee: PHANTOM OF...

On the wall next to the locker room door were three categories of bathhouse rules: NAKEDNESS, SEX, BEHAVIOR.

NAKEDNESS was allowed, even encouraged, in the showers, dressing, steam and sauna rooms, and the private berths. Towels, shorts, or robes were required inside the television and recreation areas.

SEX was prohibited anywhere in the baths. Incarnations of this rule were repeated down the length of the sign:

NO SEX ANYWHERE IN THE WEYBOSSET, BUSTER.

NO FUCKING OR BLOWING IN THE SPA.

NO GOING-DOWN ON THE PREMISES.

DON'T THINK OF SCREWING HERE.

NO HEAVY TIT WORK. NO SUCKING.

NO RIMMING. NO GLORY-HOLING.

NO WATER SPORTS. NO GOLDEN SCREW.

NO PRINCETON RUB. NO FIST-FUCK.

TODO ACTO PUBLICO SEXUAL ESTA PROHIBIDO.

In a diagonal line across the sign someone had scrawled "in your dreams."

Under the heading BEHAVIOR were prohibitions against shooting or smoking drugs, imbibing alcoholic beverages, unwelcome touching, loud voices, aggressive overtures, both verbal and physical. Against the wall below the movie-size posters of the house rules was a long table offering postcards of naked men on the front and suggestions for safe-sex practices on the back. In the center was a goldfish bowl filled with condoms.

Above the locker-room door was a hand-carved sign with facing profiles of two Gene Kelly look-alikes wearing *Anchors Aweigh* white caps and the gold letters SAILORS printed between them.

The locker room was lit so brightly that my eyes hurt when I first walked in. In the area closest to the showers a dim corridor led to the other rooms. Raised carpeted blocks lined the bottom rows of lockers. The odor of steam intensified and combined with a musty carpet smell. The room looked empty. I found my locker in the last row across a wall-length mirror and near the showers. I sat on the carpeted block and put the towel around my neck and tried to rub the stiffness from it. I faced my reflection and couldn't believe that while everything was coming unhinged, I sat in the baths and all that mattered was the certainty of sex. I wanted a drink.

The longer I looked the more surprised I was by how unchanged I appeared. While I watched my reflection, events and people from the past two days flashed by in my mind, stroboscopic, but I seemed undisturbed, as if I were someone else, looking at another life. I saw the Celtic cross of the bartender at the Slaughter, heard Jamie singing "Bye, Bye, Miss American Pie," felt Stephen Hart shooting cum inside me. I heard Chelsea barking at the package on the front stoop. There was the trick squatting on the toilet in O'Hare's bathroom. I heard Roger saying something about calamari. I envisioned blood dripping down the steam pipe in the old lady's apartment. I pictured someone named Sam breaking Stephen's rib. I watched Sarah pick up pieces of Styrofoam packing and heard Jared warn against cruising. I imagined the detective taking the handcuffs from Stephen's crystal bowl and dropping them into a plastic evidence bag. I saw the AZT and Homer Simpson. Yet everything was far away, as if none of it involved me. I wanted a whiskey. What brought my attention squarely back to the bathhouse was the young man with the Spiderman tattoo. He was standing beside me, his cock close enough for me to touch with my tongue.

"Did you notice my blue hankie when you came in?" he asked.

"I did."

"Robin's-egg blue means I want my cock sucked."

I didn't answer, but I was glad he was aroused. I watched his cock slowly grow until its tip was level with my eyes. His balls tightened between his thighs, smooth and muscular.

"I've got more hankies in my locker. Maybe you're into a different color," he said, stepping in front of me. I could see his bare ass in the mirror. I thought, *He's too young to be Sam.*

He opened the locker next to mine. The clerk had decided to put us side by side—mates, the guy's idea of a joke or an act of kindness. Out of an inside pocket of his black leather coat, tattoo man pulled a fistful of hankies.

"Do you know the codes?" he asked.

"Not a clue," I said. *Jesus, I'm flirting.* It was a relief.

"They save a lot of courting time and, at the end of a night, I don't go home disappointed. Take this greenish blue one. Know what it's saying?

"Couldn't even guess," I said.

"*Soixante-neuf,*" he said in a silly feminine French accent.

"Cute," I said.

"And this mustard one means I'm looking for a big cock. Anything to offer?"

I didn't answer him.

"Don't play so coy, or else I'll wave this fuchsia one in your face and *you'd be in for a spankin',*" he said.

I shook my head, not really disapproving.

"More dangerous?" he asked, holding up a navy blue hankie with white spots. "Come at me unprotected, baby."

I smiled, let a few beats pass.

"I think I'll go wander around the baths," he finally said.

He put the hankies into his coat pocket.

"Maybe I'll just wear this orange one around my wrist, orange like the sunshine, anything goes. Maybe we'll meet inside."

"Maybe," I said, after he turned, in time for him to hear before he disappeared into the showers.

Another man had arrived and opened his locker at the end of our row. He took off a boater's rain parka, a bright yellow one with a hood, and put it inside. He didn't look at me. Maybe *he* was the killer.

I watched him undress, secretively catching glimpses, while I took off my clothes and put them inside my locker. He was in his forties, too. Thick, wavy black hair. A strong chest and a bigger stomach than showed inside his shirt, but he wasn't fat. His legs were muscular and hairy, his ass still youthful. He slipped into a pair of red flip-flops, put a towel around his waist, and walked into the showers.

I waited until I heard the shower shut off before I went inside. When I breathed in the disinfectant in the air, I could taste it in my throat. My eyes itched. I decided not to shower. My towel was just big enough to fold the ends together around my waist—the cheap cloth felt thin and rough, and little cotton BBs from so many bleachings rubbed against my thighs like sandpaper.

The corridor to the inner sanctum of the bathhouse—the Jacuzzi, sauna, steam room, and the berths—was dimly lit by small low-wattage ceiling bulbs and tiny eye-shaped floor lights like the ones in movie theaters and airplanes. I stood for what seemed a long time before the opening to the hallway and thought about getting dressed. I saw the steam room door open and smelled the metallic air as it rushed into the corridor. Someone—naked—flitted into view and disappeared into the dim hallway. I decided to open the vault-like door and step inside the mass of vapor.

It was hot and so thick with steam that I couldn't see more than a few inches. Less than a foot from the door I had to stop to get my bearings. I heard water shooting from a hose and setting off steam bursts at several points on the ceiling. When the hissing streams abated, shapes emerged, first just flesh in the clearing patches, then parts of bodies—a shoulder, knees, and calves of someone sitting down, an ass bent over as if someone was doing a hands-to-toes exercise. Eventually the clearing air uncovered faces and whole bodies awash in rivulets of sweat. A congregation of naked men emerged like gods in the ancient baths. Because I had just arrived, most eyes turned on me, some just for a quick glance.

There were about a dozen men. They sat on tile blocks that lined the walls. A few stood in the center of the room near me, their cocks relaxed in the heat. Someone seated on a block put his hand on the thigh of the man beside him and smiled—his mouth was red and wet and looked like a wound. I turned and left.

I walked farther into the bathhouse, to the dark labyrinthine berths. The smell of sex was unmistakable.

There were no ceiling lights, only the small eye-shaped floor bulbs and the red glare cast from the zigzag wall neon. The area was divided into a creepy network of corridors lined with ceilingless cells. From above, it must have looked like a maze for laboratory rats.

Shadowy naked figures with towels dangling from their hands or wrapped around necks moved in what appeared, at first, a desultory manner. Except for a few wary newcomers, the men wandering from corridor to corridor knew what waited behind a door left ajar. Inside the berths no one spoke. I knew the sex would be joyless and ecstatic, and for that time nothing else would matter. Not even the danger of finding him naked and ready to kill.

In one room was a lumbering mass of a man. In another, two or three men huddled together on a block table, more like a bier than a bed. I entered the first empty berth and closed the door just far enough to leave a slit for an eye to see in. A stale semen smell suffused the space. In the corner was a silver condom wrapper. Nearby a wad of tissue paper lay in a slant of light cast by a floor bulb and looked like a small white dove. I rolled my towel into a pillow and placed it at the end of the wooden bunk. No mattress or cushion— just the hard wood surface. I was a Capuchin monk preparing for sleep in his catacomb monastery. All around me were statues carved from bones of dead monks.

I heard the sound of footsteps stopping. I looked sideways and saw an eye in the slit. The eye quickly disappeared. Footsteps recommenced, softer and softer, until they were gone. I thought, *Maybe he's really here, and he's come to kill me. Maybe he's the man in the boater's rain parka, someone from the steam room, not the goofy hankie-code guy.*

I lay down on the bunk and placed the rolled-up towel under my neck and head. I was tired and gave myself to the dark and rancid air. The whiskey on my breath was all that was familiar. I thought of being dead. I shut my eyes and for a while didn't think about anything. Then I tried to imagine the killer who might be named Sam and calls himself Buddy. I pictured Stephen Hart flat on his back like this but inside a body bag on a gurney on his way to the morgue.

The door opened just enough for someone to slip in. I kept my eyes closed. I heard the door shut, tight this time. I counted his footsteps—*one, two, three*—before he reached the edge of the bunk and knelt. One of his arms slid softly across my stomach, and he curled his hand under my ass and left it there. His other hand slithered up the inside of my leg, and he rested that arm against my thigh while he closed his hand over my balls. His breaths were steady and rhythmic like the sound of sex itself. The hankie tied to his wrist tickled. When I was in his arms, he leaned forward and went down on me.

■

I had become a spectator to my own family. When I stood outside the kitchen door, I wasn't thinking about the mess I'd caused. I didn't feel guilty, no hint of loss. I wasn't really drunk. I just wondered how it happened that I didn't belong there anymore.

It was a little after 8. I watched Sarah at the kitchen table. She was sipping wine from a juice glass and drawing something in one of my 9-by-4-inch reporter's notebooks—probably an impromptu sketch for an addition to an old house she was designing. She had the knack of turning idle time into something productive. I envied her. For her, everything run-down could be transformed into something beautiful. Everything could be restored. She wasn't a fraud like me. What would she do when she learned she was in the middle of something so unexpectedly terrible? And realized it was all my fault.

I waited at the back door and watched her sketch. She turned page after page, thinking intently in the way that usually ends with a characteristic look of satisfaction, hard-earned and indisputable. When I walked in, she became annoyed.

"What's happened?" she said.

"I've been working. I should have called. Didn't I say I'd be late?"

"Melanie said you left the newsroom hours ago. Jesus, you stink of whiskey. Is that all you do these days? Drink and hide things. You lied about the AP."

"I didn't lie."

"You said the call from Roger wasn't important. What's going on? Why didn't you say anything about the AP?"

"I had to write the column. Then Jared asked me to meet him about a case."

"So you got shit-faced in the middle of the afternoon."

"I'm not drunk."

Her voice was different from anything I'd heard before. She wasn't just worried, or angry, or hurt. She sounded completely uncertain about how she should react.

I stood behind her and massaged her neck and tried to find a way to begin to tell her everything.

"Bellemy called. He said he'd try back," she said. She made nervous markings on the pad.

"Did he say anything?"

"Just that he'd call back."

I remembered the messages I'd left for the reporters named Sam. "Anyone else call?"

"Roger, again. He couldn't believe you didn't tell me about the AP."

I leaned over and kissed her cheek. It surprised both of us, though we didn't say so.

"I better check e-mail," I said.

She took my arm and demanded, "Tell me what's wrong."

"I can't talk about it now. Trust me."

I kissed her head and was surprised how soft her hair felt. We'd shared so little intimacy for so long that kissing her like this was disarming.

She handed me something from the notebook and asked, "What's this? It fell out of your shirt pocket while I was putting it in the wash."

It was a card from the Slaughter.

"A place in Seattle. A steakhouse we went to."

The lie came so easily I was ashamed. I couldn't tell her everything before I figured out was what happening. I thought about Bellemy and wanted to call him.

"Are you in trouble? Why can't you talk to me? You're so goddamn uncommunicative. I'm sick of it."

I didn't know what to say, so I said nothing.

"Fine," she said. "Play silent on me, like you always do."

"Give me some time."

I walked to the cupboard, took out a glass, and put it down on the table. I poured some white zinfandel, which tasted like weak peach juice. She turned to me with an expectant look.

I put my hand on hers and said, "I'm tired."

It was one of the few honest emotions I'd shared in days.

"That's no excuse. Why didn't you tell us about the AP? It's as if you're resigned to failure, as if you take some kind of sick comfort in it."

I got up and poured myself a whiskey.

"And, lately, you've been drinking so much it worries me," she said.

She was nervous, talking in circles. I thought, *Jesus, I've got to do something soon.*

"You've always kept too much to yourself, but this time it's different. I'm scared."

"I didn't think getting on a list for some regional journalism award was such hot shit, and then this thing with Jared this afternoon. It's wiped me out."

"What thing with Jared?"

"I don't want to think about it now, please."

"You never talk about what's important to you anymore. You've got a faraway look that says, *How the hell does she think she can help?* I'm tired of it, Dan."

She was right. I thought, *I'll tell her this: For as long as I can remember I've been hiding from myself. The Slaughter's no steakhouse, it's a gay bar in Seattle. I loved a man I met there just for one night and now he's dead.* That would be a start. I thought about the hankie-code guy going down on me in the berth an hour before and knew I couldn't tell her anything. I remembered the murderer's threats. There was too much to do to make sure the sick bastard didn't hurt Jamie and her.

I just said, "I know."

"Try to be a little *positive*," she said. "Roger and Barbara are stopping by. They're at a dinner party, and when it's over, Roger is bringing champagne to celebrate your nomination. Sometime after 10, he thought. He said he'd call first."

Her word choice threw me. Someday soon, a doctor would say, "I'm sorry, you're positive." I'd forgotten about the AZT. The pills are still inside my desk.

Sarah got up and faced me. I hoped she wouldn't smell the baths.

"Did you eat?"

"I had some cheese and crackers with Jared." The habit of telling small, unnecessary lies was almost a reflex.

"There are some raviolis from Federal Hill. They're in the oven. We'll have a quick dinner before they come."

"I better clean up, take a shower."

"Jamie's angry, too. It's bad enough you bagged the exhibit."

"I'll set it straight with her." *Straight:* another word that made me nervous. I recalled Fitzgerald wondering how his crackup started: *an egocentric hypersensitivity to words?* "Where's she now?" I asked.

"With Aidan. It's their rave night at the Armada."

Good, I thought, *she'll be safe with him.*

"I'm sorry, Sarah."

"These days I can't figure you out." Her voice, though, was regaining confidence. She wanted to believe the day was returning to something she could understand.

"Give me 15 minutes."

"I'll open some good wine," she said, making little half-moons in the notebook, without raising her head when she spoke.

I went to the study and tried to reach Bellemy. He wasn't home. I left a message that sounded more urgent than I wanted it to. I thought, *He must be suspicious by now and he'd be in danger too, if the killer finds out he's been helping me. I'll have to warn him.*

When I was walking upstairs, I heard Sarah open the china cabinet and put down plates on the table. Usually, she hummed a '60s song when she prepared for dinner. I stopped on the stairs and listened. All I heard were knives and forks clanking as she lifted them from the cutlery drawer.

■

The shower didn't absolve me the way it usually did when I came home with the smell and taste of a man on my body. I rubbed oatmeal soap all over. After the orange-hankied guy had gone down on me, he spread his body over mine. There'd been enough light to see his Spiderman tattoo when he thrust himself forward and back. He tried to turn me over, but I resisted. He tried to put his cock into my mouth, but I wouldn't surrender. So he rubbed it against my face and up and down my chest until he spread cum from my neck to my navel—a Princeton rub. When he was finished, he left. I stayed flat on my back almost an hour more. I think I might have even slept.

After I dressed, I sat on the bed a few minutes and didn't have a good idea what to do next. *He said he had plans for me.* I thought about Sarah's distress, how much easier everything would have been if we'd divorced years ago. I imagined Jamie dancing in a kind of mystical frenzy at the Armada and wondered whether she'd understand. I wanted to love being gay, wanted the lies and boozy sex to end. I thought about Jared. I wanted him, too. Somehow I had to find a way out of this. I'd start by telling Sarah everything. She'd see the danger, and we'd deal with it together. I wanted a drink.

■

It was almost 9:30 when we sat down to eat, and Sarah was still tense.

"You deserve it," she said.

"What?" I asked, surprised that she might be lashing

back at me, and in rare vindictive mood, relishing it.

"What do you think? The AP," she said.

"I'm not so sure."

"We've been married 20 years, and I'm still surprised by how hard you are on yourself."

She'd opened a bottle of expensive merlot and poured me a glass. I didn't have an answer, but it didn't matter because she had more to say.

"I wish you could see how lucky you are. You have a daughter who adores you, a wife with the patience of Job, work you love, and still you mope like some palooka."

"You just learned that word this morning."

She laughed. "So what?"

She held up her glass and said, "To our family, Dan."

I thought, *She doesn't know how hard she's making this.*

"Our family," I said.

She cut a piece of ravioli and ate it. I understood that this might be the last time that she'd be sitting down with me to dinner, and the thought of her trying so hard to be happy made it harder to tell her.

"It's been a long time since I told you I love you," I said.

"You aren't gushy."

"I'm sorry. Two people in love should speak of it more."

I thought, *This isn't the best way to begin.*

"You like being Mr. Taciturn when it comes to your feelings. I've accepted it. Sometimes, like lately, it's harder than others."

"I'm sorry."

"Say it again and I'll throw a ravioli in your face. *Sorry*—You can do better than that. *Sorry*'s no valentine."

I thought of the hankie-code man with CARNAGE written across his hand on top of me, and I was speechless.

I got up and poured a whiskey. I drank it and poured another. I was the kind of drinker who drank to hide. I never lost control. I escaped.

"How many did you have today? My wine's not good enough?" She was sounding nervous again.

"I'm just uneasy."

"You're going to get offers." At first, I was surprised and stupidly thought she might have been talking about love.

"What?"

"If you get the AP award, other newspapers will want to hire you."

I didn't say anything.

"With Jamie going to college, there's no reason we have to stay in Providence."

She was looking for a new beginning. I felt sorry for her; she didn't have a clue.

"Something's wrong," I said, so somberly that she didn't hear because the doorbell rang just as I said it. I'd been ready to tell her everything.

"They're here," she said and walked to the front door.

"We tried calling," I heard Roger say in the foyer. "But your line's been busy for the past half hour."

"No one's been on the telephone," Sarah said, taking their coats and flopping them on the bench across from the door.

"Funny," Barbara said. "Maybe I had the wrong number."

"Where's Dan?" Roger asked.

"He's in the kitchen sulking," Sarah said. "Dan, your fan club's arrived." Her voice sounded so carefree I wanted to disappear.

Roger put his arms around me and offered his congratulations.

He'd grown up in Queens, a reporter for the *Daily News*

before he took a job heading the investigative team at the *Record* in the late '60s. Ten years later, as editor in chief, he hired me, a kid right out of Notre Dame whose only experience in journalism was a column I wrote for the underground paper at the university. He decided to put me on the night-cop beat. He said to me before my first shift, "You've got to see and hear before you understand a goddamn thing, son." I remembered thinking that my father had never called me "son."

Roger led the way into the family room. He didn't like formality, preferring a seat in the La-Z-Boy, his shoes off and feet elevated, as if he were in his own home. Barbara was his second wife. When they met, she'd been the *Record*'s religion writer—a former nun whose fame, unfairly, rested on her excommunication from the Roman Catholic Church. She'd written a series on abortion. Now she was the director of the local chapter of Planned Parenthood. I remembered seeing her on *Phil Donahue*—some caller had said she was a modern scourge of the Catholic Church. She had a voice like cashmere. When a priest in the audience called her a baby murderer, she stood up, looked him in the eyes, and said, so softly that the microphones nearly didn't pick it up, "You, sir, can burn in hell."

For a moment, their presence made me think nothing had changed.

"Break out the champagne," Roger said. "We've got a prize winner." He sat and grinned.

"Dan reminded me that most of the people short-listed for a prize don't win," Sarah said.

"It must be his Russian side," Barbara said. "There's disappointment waiting behind every door."

"It's not a prize," Roger said. "It's an award, something a writer earns, not wins."

My attention drifted and I drank more whiskey.

"He didn't tell me about it. I heard from Roger," Sarah said.

I stood in the no-man's land between the family room and the kitchen. I didn't say a word while they talked about what they'd decided was my state of "perpetual dissatisfaction." Secretly, I liked the description.

"Perpetual dissatisfaction," Roger said. "It's like one of those realms of religious limbos, you know, like purgatory."

I pictured Purgatory Chasm. *Perpetual dissatisfaction. Maybe I should tell them about my recurring dream. The one that's always left me desolate: Two men pass me along a riverbank. They're holding hands and are happy. What does this group know about unhappiness?*

"Hey, columnist, make yourself useful and get us four champagne glasses," Roger said.

"Three," I said, preparing for reentry. "I'm drinking whiskey."

Sarah gave me a look and followed me to the kitchen to gather up cheese and olives.

"They just came from dinner. It's after 10," I said. When her back was turned, I drank another Bushmills.

"Don't irritate me. Just get the glasses and try to have a good time."

Jesus, I thought, *maybe the killer's e-mailed me. Why didn't I check?*

I said, "You get the glasses. I'll be right there. I forgot I promised to make a call."

She looked irritated but just said, "Don't take too long."

In the study, I clicked on the PC and checked the mail. Nothing. Not even one from Bellemy. I'd given him the address. He'd know it would have been more private than a phone call. I wondered why he wanted to talk.

When I got back to the family room, the phone rang.

Sarah filled the last glass with champagne and answered it.

"Roger, the phone's for you. It's Andy."

"Son-of-a bitch," he said. "What's so important the goddamn managing editor can't handle it?"

He took the phone and listened to an eleventh-hour crisis being thrown in his lap.

"Delay the presses a half-hour and run whatever you get by then on page 3. For Christ's sake, it's Easter Sunday, and we aren't going to wave body parts in readers' faces when they wake up."

He didn't say goodbye.

"There's been a murder at the bathhouse on Weybosset," he said. "We might have our own Dahmer or Gacy."

I knocked over a champagne glass.

"Get a kitchen towel," Sarah told me. "It's spilling on the rug." She said, "I haven't heard about any serial murders."

"Remember the priest who was beaten near the railroad tracks a while ago?" Barbara asked.

I returned and wiped up the champagne.

"He wasn't killed," I said.

"No, but he was lucky," Roger said. "Later, there was a vicious murder with some evidence linking it to the priest. That kid who was tied to the piling in the harbor. He'd been slashed over and over. We found out the cops didn't release all of the details. He'd been tricking by the railroad tracks for months. They said they didn't want to spook the killer and make him run. Can you believe it? Someone's targeting gays, and the cops don't go public. The bastard chopped off the kid's foot and pinned a used condom to his chest. Apparently, the priest had a badge, too. You don't want to hear anymore about it. Not tonight."

Jesus, I thought, *Jared never told me about the condoms. What if he knew about Stephen Hart and didn't tell me?*

I was visibly shaken and asked, "What happened at the bathhouse?" I could see Sarah was trying to figure out why I was so upset.

"The police aren't giving us much. Andy said he thinks the victim was a local john, young, someone who hangs around the clubs and cruising spots," Roger said. "The I-team's on it. They're talking to detectives. The bigger story's going to run next week. But we're reporting the possibility of a gay serial thing tomorrow. Christ, on Easter Sunday."

"Nobody told me."

"You were away. Besides, the I-team wants to play this one real close until the main story runs."

"They hear of any similar murders anywhere else?" I asked.

"Nope. He's made Providence his home, as far as we know. Lucky us."

I thought, *Screw the I-team. They didn't find out about the firefighter's murder. Crap investigators.*

I went to the kitchen and poured another whiskey. I shivered and wondered, *What the fuck is happening?*

The phone rang. I yelled, "I've got it." It was Bellemy.

He told me he'd found a connection between the firefighter's murder and the slaying of a Cambodian kid in Providence. Enger had been talking to a Providence investigator and planned to fly out Monday. Bellemy said he still couldn't find out anything more about the reporters named Sam, but he suspected I knew more than I was saying and maybe had something to do with the murders.

"That's crazy," I said.

"Who's kidding who? You expect me to believe this shit about some guy writing an out-of-the-beat story about marriage?"

"I told you this is personal."

"That's not enough, Dan. There's a serial involved. You're hiding something."

"Fuck you," I said, and hung up.

I drank the whiskey and decided I had to get out of the house. I took a pint from the back of the liquor shelf, behind the old bottles of after-dinner drinks we never used, and put the whiskey in my pocket. I had to get out of the house and figure out what to do. I felt dizzy and drawn into the night air.

"Hey, we're here to toast to our columnist; the murderous city can wait," Barbara said.

"Dan, get in here," Roger shouted.

Sarah asked, "What the hell is wrong with you tonight?"

The sharpness in her voice surprised everyone.

I was back, standing in the hideout between the kitchen and family room and thinking about the black berth. I was remembering being sucked.

"What's wrong?" Barbara asked. "You're not happy."

"I'm worn out," I said. "I'm working on something tough."

"What?" Roger said. "What's rattling you like this?"

"I don't want to talk the story out."

"Secretive is more like it," Roger said.

Sarah knew I was lying and was visibly angry.

"The toast," Barbara said.

I drank some champagne before anyone said a word. Everything seemed like it was caving in. I thought, *They're here, Jamie's at her rave with Aidan, everyone's going to be OK.*

"Excuse me," I said and walked away.

I was at the door when Sarah shouted, "Don't you dare leave."

"Sorry," I said, barely loud enough for her to hear.

prospect terrace

In my rearview mirror, I watched her at the front of the driveway waving for me to come back inside. She looked like she had just stepped into a silent avalanche. I tried to convince myself I'd left to find him, but the truth was— unbelievably so—I went out hunting. As I drove away, the streetlamps made neighbors' yards seem inescapably real, and for an instant, I almost forgot the mess I'd made. I fished out the pint and took another drink. I remembered the doctor when I passed his white stucco house—the place lit as if he expected his dead wife to return at any time. He was only 35 years old, an internist who looked like he was used to seeing ghosts. He'd told me I needed to bring down my blood pressure. "Borderline high: It takes a toll on a heart," he said. He should know. In the car passing his house, I thought, *He's handsome.*

When I turned onto Hope Street, I noticed the bartender locking the door to the bistro Rue de l'Espoir. He was young,

20-something, and his eyes were blue and beautiful. I remembered them from the times he'd handed me a Bushmills. His name was Jonathan, and he'd studied Nathaniel Hawthorne and Herman Melville. *He's handsome, too,* I thought. He never guessed that when I climbed into bed, where Sarah was already asleep, I sometimes dreamed about him, his thick light hair tucked under my chin. I dreamed about the doctor, too. When other gay men dreamed, I wondered whether they dreamed the way I did. When they slept, did they undress men they met outside their dreams?

As I turned onto Benevolent Street, the buildings of Brown University emerged like the opening pan in a movie about love and loss: red-brick residence halls with stately chimney stacks and slate roofs in tree-lined quadrangles. I passed the deep blue and brown and red colonial houses— departments of geology, classical languages, Judaic studies. The painted Victorian ladies—*Like Stephen Hart's in Seattle,* I thought. More university offices, apartments. A neighborhood of consequence and comfort. Its beauty reached far back into the past. In summer the blue jays spoke in Greek; at night skunks pored over musty manuscripts.

Sometimes I drove down these paths after 2 in the morning, when they were empty except for young couples returning from Fellini's, the late-night pizzeria on Wickenden. The occasional single young man, who would turn to look at a passing driver. If he didn't turn away at once, he might smile, maybe nod. Sometimes he looked long enough to show he was searching too. Enough to signal a driver, usually an older man, someone like me, sometimes me, out late at night, almost somnambulant, looking for sex.

I circled back and stopped at the light on Hope and

George. I felt I was in the car dreaming about being in the car. A man carrying a white chocolate bunny the size of a two-year-old walked past. It had two York mints for eyes, round and black. He smiled innocently and disappeared into a narrow alleyway between houses. It would be Easter Sunday soon. On this night 2,000 years ago, Jesus was lying in a tomb, alone with desert grubs and scorpions, waiting for dawn when the boulders would part. And here, on this night, I was out hunting. I picked up the pint from the seat and took a drink.

George Street was empty except for a university security guard on his rounds entering one of the academic offices. He didn't seem to notice me meandering through the campus roads: Charlesfield and Benefit, John and Manning, Power and Williams, some of the houses older than America. At the corner of College and Prospect, someone in a black wool coat appeared in the moonlight. He looked at me as I drove past. I circled the block with feline patience, and when I returned to the corner, he was gone. I pulled to the side of the road and sat in the car to see if he, or maybe someone else, would walk by. In my rearview I saw two young men in Patriots jackets headed up College Street, and when they passed the car, I smiled.

"Go fuck yourself, fag," one said.

The other one took a stone from his pocket and hurled it into my windshield, which didn't shatter but opened a crack about an arm's length across it. They cheered and bolted.

Jesus, I thought, *what am I doing out like this?* I was about to go back home when the night walker in the black coat returned. He crossed the street and looked at the cracked windshield.

"I saw them throw it," he said.

Immediately I knew I wasn't leaving. There wouldn't be

a need for a negotiation because his voice revealed he wasn't worried about whether he could trust me. Sometime later when he learned about the serial gay killings, maybe he'd wonder about his recklessness. But what mattered to him then was his desire for sex—blind and overpowering like mine.

I looked around the street.

"Don't worry. They're not coming back. I've seen them before. Once they hit a target, they're done for the night. Afraid, I guess, the cops might be watching," he said.

"That's never happened to me before."

"Lucky, I guess. So, what's up?"

"I could use some company."

He smiled—not at all nervously.

"I'd like to walk. Prospect Terrace is a block away." He pointed to the right. "A great view *and* a blow job."

I turned off the engine and got out of the car. I reached back in for the pint of whiskey. The night was warmer than it had been all day. The fog had long ago retreated and the sky looked wired with starlight. I knocked over an empty beer can on the curb that rattled onto the street. It was the only sound around.

"You said you've seen those guys."

"Maybe not them, but others. There's been a lot of bashings on the hill lately," he said. He crossed the street ahead of me and waited there while I locked the car door.

We didn't say anything else until we reached the park where Roger Williams is buried on a hill overlooking downtown. The compulsion that kept sending me out into the night stole everything, and I moved like someone sleepwalking. "This is it," he said, inside the terraced park near the statue, which was nearly three stories high—its massive arms outstretched from its perch at the edge of the hill. He led the way to an iron bench next to steps that descended to the base of the statue.

I thought about how young he was—maybe 20 years old—and wondered why he was even interested. I felt momentarily sad, and thought, *He's in the closet, too.*

"I love it here," he said.

"I'm Daniel."

"Let's be anonymous."

I offered him some Bushmills.

"Sure," he said, before taking a swill. He coughed and said, "strong stuff."

I took one, too. The bottle was only half empty. Surprisingly, I wasn't drunk. I was just on my way somewhere else.

"Are you at the university?" I asked.

He didn't say anything, and I worried that he'd leave. I touched his thigh.

"Let's go down there." He rose from the bench and signaled with a hand to follow down the steps.

When I reached him, he pushed me against the concrete pedestal with a force that hurt and excited me. He looked at me for a long time, and I was surprised that I wasn't afraid. *He doesn't have a knife and he's going to kiss me. He's too young and beautiful to be a killer.*

He held my shoulders against the concrete and lifted a knee so that it pressed, softly, into my groin.

"So what does it take to get you hard?" he asked.

His kiss tasted like tobacco. He knelt and unbuckled my belt, unfastened and unzipped my khakis, and tore my boxers down to my ankles. While he sucked me, I watched the night unfold in Providence: Streetlights shimmered on the river winding under stone bridges, some Hell's Angels raced down North Main, and a squirrel on an electric wire, almost close enough to touch, paused before running off. When he was finished, I felt the tip of something sharp against my thigh. It was the blade of a Swiss Army knife.

"Your wallet," he said, moving the blade closer to my balls and reaching into the back pocket of my pants.

I thought, *He is the killer.*

He took the cash and my ATM card. "What's the password?" he asked calmly, as if he's been through this before. "I'll take the limit tonight and then destroy it."

After I gave him the numbers, he said, "These better be right, or I'll find you." Then he shot his knee up my groin so hard I buckled over.

By the time I was back on my feet and pulled up my pants, he was gone. I slid down the pedestal and sat on the narrow walk, my knees bent against my chest, the soles of my shoes flat against the iron fence. "Sometimes I feel like a motherless child"—I sang, rocking slightly, aware of the ridiculousness. *Lucky,* I thought. *He could have been the killer but instead he's some kid who wanted some cock and cash. Maybe it's the whiskey that's fucked me up so bad.*

The city at night flickered through the lattice design of the wrought-iron fence. Buildings were silhouettes, not piles of bricks and mortar. I thought, *Fuck providence. There's just luck, or no luck at all. It's rotten luck his condom broke inside me. Stupid luck someone sent me his penis. Bad luck the kid held a knife against my balls. What do I have to do with any of it? I read this in the paper: Doesn't anyone understand? When a man fucks you, it's like sitting in a café during a war. You pretend the conflict doesn't exist.*

I thought, *I never used to think this way. Jesus, what if he wants to kill everyone who tricks with me?*

Sarah would be waiting for an explanation this time. There'd be a reckoning. I'd tell the truth about the Slaughter.

I'd tell her about the box with his penis in it. I'd explain about the bathhouse. I'd show her the murderer's messages. I'd tell her about Sam the batterer and Bellemy, who knows I'm lying. I'd tell her about the detective flying out to Providence. I'd explain Jared didn't tell me he knew about the firefighter's murder and the condoms pinned to the stiffs' chests. *Jesus,* I thought, *maybe he thinks I'm the guy. Maybe he thinks I'm covering for someone.* I wouldn't tell Sarah about the night in the cruiser nearly 20 years ago. She'd be speechless for a while, and then I wouldn't know what she'd say. I wouldn't tell her about the park. I couldn't tell her this: a kid going down on and stealing from me in the middle of everything.

I thought about Jamie and started to cry. She'd be home from the rave, asleep in her bed, a Critical Mass bracelet loose on her wrist, the music—Lola, Chicken Lips, Anagram—still spinning in her dreams. She'd wake up in the morning and I'd have to tell her how I've lied for so long. I'd have to tell her about the bastard threatening us. I'd have to watch her world fall out from under her.

I climbed the steps and sat on the iron bench. My groin ached. A few cars slowed when they passed the park, but none stopped. It was just after midnight, a lull in cruising, too late for men already home asleep, too early for others buying time until the bars and clubs closed for the night. I thought of finishing the whiskey, but decided to leave it. I thought, *How did I get here? Forty-two years old in a park after midnight, where not too long ago a young man was sucking and assaulting me in the dark and open air? And Jesus, the real maniac might be watching even now.*

I was sorry I wasn't drunk enough to stop thinking and looked down at the grass. Not too far away, lit by gas lamplight, was a gathering of slugs, about 10, thick brown fleshy things, each the size of a finger but fatter, with black rectangular marks; some marks were long, others short, like penciled-in boxes on a test or a lottery card. They were inching along the ground.

I'd never tricked with so many men before. I could have counted four men, maybe, in a year. Stephen Hart was easy to explain, but why the others? *I'll just sit here in the dark until I understand.*

A car parked along the curb. Its engine whirred and then shut off. I didn't turn around to see because I didn't want to encourage anyone. I wanted the dark for myself.

My hearing seemed heightened, almost canine. Someone got out, the sound of a single car door closing, deliberately. I thought of a man lying in his blood in the bathhouse. Would I recognize him? Was he the tattooed man? The red-sandaled boater? The man touching his toes inside the steam room? It occurred to me that the murderer might have opened the car door. His footsteps still audible when he reached the grass. *Don't worry,* I thought, almost speaking the words aloud as if that would make them true. *It's another man cruising. He'll notice I want to be left alone, and he'll go over to the other bench.* I heard the sound of keys or pocket change. His hand on my shoulder felt like a detonation. I gulped, a fistful of air striking my diaphragm.

"I was on my way to your house," Jared said.

He sat down.

"You scared the shit out of me. How'd you know I was here?"

When I turned to see him, my knee touched his leg.

"I called and Sarah said you'd walked out. She was scared. So I thought I'd look around the cruising places, and I saw your car parked on George. The PRESS 5 plate makes you easy to spot."

I moved my leg away.

"She asked what case we were working on. She said you'd been acting strange and wouldn't talk about it. Why'd you tell her we were working on something?"

"Quit fucking with me, Jared. You know what's going on."

"I know you've been lying to me."

"You think I killed them all," I said.

"Where'd you go after you left me this afternoon?" he asked.

The start of an interrogation, I thought.

"You know where I went, and you think I killed that bathhouse trick."

"What I know is you've gotten yourself into something crazy bad, and you're not telling me."

I looked away toward the city. The headlights of an Amtrak train snaked around the statehouse before disappearing underground. I wasn't entirely in the moment. Providence was swimming, just hours before the resurrection, almost luminescent under the night sky. I wanted a drink.

"Why'd you tell the Weybosset clerk you were a minister?"

"Closeted men hide," I said. I wanted to say, *You should know,* but I didn't.

"The stiff is Bob Bordeo, 26, from the South End. He's been tricking downtown for a couple of years. He was cut up in one of the private rooms. The clerk said you walked in right behind him. He gave you lockers side by side."

"Christ, not the hankie-code man."

"We found a bunch in his coat pocket. But he's missing a hand."

I looked at him and said, "You really think I killed him."

"He was still alive after you left. The clerk said you took off a little after 8 and he saw the guy buy a soda at about

8:30. Sarah said you were home by then. You didn't kill him."

Cops see everything in one straight line. What the fuck do they know? I wanted a drink. I remembered my cock inside the guy's mouth and wished he wasn't dead. I saw his Spiderman tattoo and the clerk's head bobbing into view in the office porthole.

"If you know I didn't kill him, why the grilling?" I asked.

"There's something going down here and you're involved and the only reason I'm telling you this is I believe you didn't kill anyone. And I think you're in more trouble than you know."

"You don't know shit about trouble."

"That kid I saw you talking to by the tracks a while ago? He's the kid who was sliced up and tied to a submerged piling in the harbor 10 days ago. The firefighter in Seattle and the guy tonight—you think these are all coincidences?"

I understood he was trying to help, but his voice gained an intensity that made me nervous.

I said, "You didn't tell me that you knew about the firefighter."

"I wasn't sure what to think about that situation. I had to test you."

Situation—another word cops use when they mean a whole lot more than they're saying.

"I don't like being tested by someone I trust. Jesus, I don't know what's happening."

"You know more than you think." His voice sounded detached, as if it came from an invisible speaker in the air— his detective's voice.

"Let's start with the bathhouse," he said.

"He wore an orange hankie around his wrist. When he went

down on me, it tickled." Just telling Jared this felt like a crime.

"You weren't the only one."

"What's that mean?"

"There were others. We interviewed everyone. Queens talk." He shot me a look and said, "Most of them."

He let the criticism sink in and then continued. "The medical examiner has taken swabs from all of his orifices. A lot of company. A regular fuck-witted Athenian holiday. I hope it was worth it."

He sounded almost disgusted.

I said, "Jesus, the kid."

"What kid? The Cambodian? He's already in the ground."

"The guy tonight. He stole my money and went down on me over there." I pointed toward the stairs leading to the stone pedestal.

"Fuck, another trick?"

"He's killing them," I said. "The guy in the bathhouse proves he's killing men I trick with."

"What do you mean he stole your money?"

"He had a knife. After he blew me, he took cash and my ATM card from my wallet." I started to shake.

Jared cupped a hand around my arm and told me to keep myself together.

"What's he look like?" he asked.

"About 19, 20. Almost six feet, good build, not skinny, not fat. Black hair, glasses with thick black frames. like Buddy Holly's. He was wearing a long black wool coat, kind of Goth-looking, no piercings."

Jared got on his cell and called for a few cruisers to come to the park.

"What else are you hiding?" he asked, astonished at what he didn't know about me.

"There's a columnist out west. His name's Bellemy. He knows I'm involved somehow."

"Enger mentioned him."

"You know about Enger? You hid this too."

"I'm running an investigation, and you're part of it. Don't you understand. If I were someone else, you would have been hauled in by now or maybe even locked up."

Why am I responding like he isn't trying to help?

"I called Hart's house Friday night and hung up on Enger."

"He told me. You've heard of caller I.D., star-69. It's easy to find out who makes a call."

"He thinks I killed Stephen."

"What he knows is that your actions are suspicious. I'm trying to convince him you're a victim here, too. So far, he's giving me some room."

"He had a lover—a married guy, a crime reporter who beat him. I think he's the killer."

"Enger didn't mentioned him."

While I was telling Jared everything that Bellemy discovered about Winchel, a few cruisers pulled up to the curb and some blues headed our way.

"Wait here," he said. "I'm going to send them looking for your guy in the park. I'll be back."

What about the condoms? How would someone in Seattle know about that part of the M.O.? Maybe the serial killer isn't Sam Winchel. Maybe the guy's from here. I fished out the pint of whiskey from my coat, drank the last swallow, and sniffed the fumes lingering in the bottle. I was sorry the hankie-code man was dead. I was sorry my wife and daughter were going to suffer. I was sorry I hadn't killed somebody, because then I could go to jail and be forgotten. I was a sorry-ass sorry excuse for a human being. I was sorry about everything and knew it wouldn't matter to anyone.

Jared returned and sat down. A cat stopped its prowling and stared.

"Did you know even a blind cat can see?" I asked.

"What the fuck," he said.

"If the nerves to the retinas are dead, degenerated right to the endings, some cats can still sense everything around them as if they still had vision."

"What's going on inside your skull?"

"Someone from Seattle probably isn't the killer."

"Why?"

"The condoms."

"Anyone could have found that information in a national crime network search. We figured it's possible someone in Seattle who knows how to access the network found the details about the Cambodian kid's murder and decided to copycat, or maybe, like you say, the serial killer could be one of ours."

"Ours?"

"Homegrown in Providence. It's possible. Or maybe someone like a reporter or a cop, anyone with access to police postings, like I said. That puts Winchel on the top of the list. One thing for sure: He isn't going to stop until he wants to or until we make him."

He was quiet for a while and then said, "Now tell me everything you know."

So I told him about Stephen Hart and the souvenir at the doorstep. I told him about Buddy and the messages and how I'd talked about Buddy at the newspaper conference. He asked me about the hankie-code man, and I told him everything I knew about him, too, which wasn't much.

I said, "In the berth, we didn't say a word. I don't even think he knew I was the same guy from the locker room. It was dark, and I was on my back looking at the ceiling when he came in. I turned my head, but all I could see was a lumbering black mass. I didn't know who he was until I felt the hankie on my skin. He had a big cock."

"*He had a big cock?* What's wrong with you? You could have been killed in that cesspool. This afternoon I warned you."

I wanted to ask Jared if I could go home with him. Tell him I was lost. I almost said, *You're so handsome I could cry.* I thought about facing Sarah and Jamie, and I wanted to disappear. I looked at him and was surprised by how remote he suddenly seemed.

"I wish your dick was as smart as you think you are," he said.

"What if this maniac decides to hurt Sarah and Jamie?"

He moved closer, more sympathetic, and said he would send an unmarked to sit outside the house. "They'll be OK," he said.

He put his arm around my shoulder. His embrace was large enough for me to sleep in.

"You didn't make this happen, but he's decided you're a part of his shit, and we're going to have to figure out why and stop him before he hurts anyone else."

I wrapped my arms around my chest like a restraint. He let me sit there in a silence for a while until, despite all the boozy mistakes I'd made, I understood I wasn't alone in this anymore. Back on his cell, he sent a car to the house.

"The watch will be there in a few minutes," he said.

"You never really believed I killed anyone," I said.

I worried he'd hesitate, but he didn't.

"You don't have the instinct for it."

I didn't answer right away, and then I said, "We've got to make sure he thinks I haven't gone to the cops."

I let my leg press against him, so lightly that he might not have noticed. He didn't move away.

"You're a cop. What if he knows we've talked?"

"He doesn't have to know you've told me anything. For all he knows, you might be a suspect. Maybe that's what he wants. When he contacts you again, if he asks about me, you lie. You say I looked for you because you were in the bathhouse log. You tell him you think the cops believe you might have killed the bathhouse trick. You try to get close to him. You say anything that gets him closer to you. You lie."

"Lying's easy. I've mastered it."

He gave me a look and said, "First, we have to figure out why he's picked you. If he's the firefighter's lover, you pissed him off. If he isn't, we need to find some other motive. He's working fast, and he wants something even more terrible than he's already gotten. My hunch is this isn't going to go on for much longer, and we're going to make sure it doesn't."

Jared said that tomorrow he'd find a way to get the techs to check my e-mails. The one at the *Record* wouldn't be so easy—"First Amendment crap," he said. He'd figure out how to get to the PC in my study without drawing the killer's suspicion

"You'd be surprised what my guys can retrieve," he said.

"Tomorrow's Easter," I said.

"Tough. We're going to have to move fast and be sharp. You look like shit. Get some sleep. In the morning you'll have a lot of explaining to do at home."

Before he got up I felt the muscle in his thigh flex against me. I didn't want to believe it was accidental. "Wait," he said. "You have my beeper and cell. Call me if he reaches you. Don't be stupid. Don't do anything he says until you talk to me."

I walked him to his car and shook his hand. It felt ridiculous.

"Thanks," I said.

"It's what I do," he said.

I nodded and tried to smile and wondered what our lives would have been if we hadn't walked away from everything we felt that night in the warehouse parking lot.

Before he drove off, he said, "Hey, when's it's over, maybe I'll throw you a goddamn coming-out party."

■

As I passed through a puddle of lamplight on the way to the car, I noticed something that looked like a cocoon. It was a used condom. I scanned the park and street to see whether someone was nearby. No one visible anywhere. I thought, *Why the condoms? Does he think he's tagging the dead? Medals, ceremonial last respects—Trojan, Kimono, Natural Lamb?* All of a sudden in the street his dead gathered. They circled me on my way back, pieces of bodies swirling in the air, everywhere and nowhere.

I sat in the car and hoped the ghosts would vanish. I pictured families inside the houses painted cobalt blue and sandstone, golden yellow and cherry, gray silk and signal red, rose and royal ivory. In the gaslight the clapboard colonials stood: a testament to everything that endures. Inside, nothing wretched ever happened. Most of the husbands loved their wives and were happy, and they shielded their children from danger. Men and women grew old together, with only the occasional hint of death shifting closer. Ancestors kept watch. The whole neighborhood reincarnated night after night, block by block, with the history of a nation still evolving until some catastrophe, natural or man-made, a hurricane or tactical nuclear weapon, would end it all. Sarah helped to restore some of the homes: a Mayan-tiled floor in a kitchen, a backyard sunroom studded with starlight, a wooden staircase spiraling like a helix, a bedroom with the aroma of heather rising to a high dreamcatcher portal.

No one threatened their tranquility. No one pried open a window and climbed into a house where a portrait of a great-great grandfather, maybe a descendant of the Colony, hung against a burgundy wall. On the way through an elegant living room, no killer walked past a small Steinway or Chickering or Wurlitzer, a metronome silent inside its ebony box. No stranger bent on harm ascended a staircase to bedrooms where a family slept, someone dreaming of a flight over the Italian Alps, someone else a swim through a school of tiger fish in the South Pacific.

I tried to imagine the kind of murderer who found his victims in dark places far from here: the corner of a urine-scented barroom after a game of pool, a parked car purring in the alleyway outside a dive's graffitied brick wall, a path near railroad tracks, a bathhouse berth.

Not tonight, not in the park on Prospect Terrace.

If he was the firefighter's lover, did he hate himself because he didn't want to love men? Or was he jealous and capable of feeling only his own maniacal self-love? Did he let his victims suck him first—did he enter them? Did he kiss with a feigned tenderness that left a lonely man disarmed? Did he know Stephen Hart had put a hand around my back and let me feel the practiced fingers of a lover sliding down the seat of my pants, pressing into the crack of my ass? Did he see starlight when it had happened to him? What was he thinking when he sliced off his lover's penis?

I tried to picture him. He was handsome. His voice was

rich and convincing, tempting and guileless. His eyes deep brown, drawing his prey's image into his blackest recesses where he began to imagine the horror he would perform. Or they were blue and beautiful, a con man's surface splendor, reflecting nothing at all. His hair was black, combed straight back on the sides, like a Spaniard's. With waves, boyish, shining, more than enough to turn away a man's suspicion. He was strong, his chest commanding. His arms were muscular. Even the dark hair filling the buttoned slits of his shirtsleeves was an enchantment. If I met him on the railroad path or at Purgatory Chasm—any clandestine place—I would want to kiss him, too. Maybe I had.

Or maybe he believed he was a failure: a freak abandoned by his family, friendless with no one to sleep beside night after night. He believed he was a rat cornered in the basement of a tenement, an outcast, an abomination. More despicable than Dahmer, who at least was loved by his mother and father; viler than Gacy, who for years played the clown for neighborhood kids; more base than Bundy, who was charming and handsome. His was a virulent self-centeredness. He was a monster. There was nothing banal about his atrocities. He beat his wife, then Stephen. The urge to harm others escalated until it pounded unspeakably in his skull. He was nothing like an ordinary man.

I wanted to hate him, but when I tried, he seemed far away, untouchable. Even more reason to hate myself for being so careless with my life and the people who trusted me. His assaults were as senseless as a twister touching down on a trailer park. And my reaction? I'd gone out hunting men. What the fuck had I become?

I recoiled from the headlights of a passing SUV. I turned the ignition key but didn't start the engine.

On the radio, excerpts from Handel's *Messiah* played in

no particular order. The soprano's voice was like a bell. I wanted to believe I was dead. She sang about a redeemer: "For now is Christ raised from the dead, the firstfruits of them that sleep." Then the music doubled back to an air from the beginning—there was the boy from Nazareth. A tenor sang, "Every valley shall be exalted, and every mountain and hill made low, the crooked straight, and the rough places plain."

I'd heard the music for the first time in Our Lady of Victory Basilica in Lackawanna when I was a boy. Above the altar, under heavy purple Lenten cloth, nothing obliterated his nakedness. No death. No resurrection. Wizened Sister Aloysius noticed me staring and made me pay for it in morning catechism. She understood I loved his stomach muscles, which disappeared into the cloth around his hips. Maybe she did, too. His flesh was like a flirtation. Years before, when he'd left Galilee, he was ridiculed, deserted by friends, scorned on his way through the green coastal plain and over desert hills to Jerusalem. In tones as solemn as death the tenor sang: "He looked for some to have pity on him, but there was no man, neither found He any to comfort him." And then, after a brief interlude, the soprano returned: "He was cut off out of the land of the living."

Later he was nailed to the cross and taken down to a tomb and prepared for the resurrection. Trumpets sounded and a bass-baritone shouted: "And the dead shall be raised incorruptible." I turned off the radio.

The dead would not rise incorruptible. The boy had been alive when his tongue was cut out before he was tied to the piling in the harbor. Had his tormentor smiled as he went about his work? Even Handel's insistent trumpeter must have known this horrible truth: No man rises incorruptible. I thought of Jesus on the cross, of dancing naked with

Stephen Hart to Louis Armstrong's "Melancholy." I started the car engine and headed home.

■

Three in the morning and all of the rooms in the house were lit, even Jamie's bedroom. A new-model sedan with tinted windows was parked across the street—the patrol Jared had sent.

At first I drove past and believed it would be better for everyone if I went to a hotel for the night. I parked outside a playground a block away. Moonlight on the plastic yellow slide made me feel desolate. I decided to call Sarah and tell her I didn't know exactly what was happening, but needed to spend the night alone to figure it out. I'd tell her the crisis had been coming on for a long time. We'd talk about everything in the morning. She'd worry and I'd tell her there would be a way for this to end without anyone getting hurt. I'd tell her not to trouble Jamie, to say I was working a story late into the night if she asked. I wouldn't tell Sarah I loved her, though I did in a way that couldn't possibly satisfy her. She'd be speechless. She wouldn't cry, but she'd understand something irreversible was happening. All emotions would empty from her for the one bare moment that follows the recognition marriage is over. She'd be standing in the kitchen with the phone to her side like someone who'd lost more than she'd believed was possible. Her silence would be my obliteration.

I took the cell phone from the glove compartment and called. Sarah answered on one ring.

"Hello," she said. "Hello. Who's there?"

I clicked off and drove home.

She appeared at the front door on the stoop where not

24 hours earlier someone had left me Stephen Hart's penis. She stood, a hand across her chest, holding her shoulder, trying to soothe what suddenly seemed a lifetime of aching. Jamie walked up behind her, straining to see how much more worry the night would blow in.

She pointed to the sedan. It was parked along the curb under the slender branches of a willow tree barely visible in light from a neighbor's garage.

"That car's been parked there for about an hour," she said.

"It's a cop," I said, looking back to the street.

"Dad, not the police," Jamie said nervously.

Sarah held her around the shoulder.

"She's terrified," she said.

We walked in and closed the door.

"What happened?"

"That's what we want to know."

Jamie said, "Someone held a gun to the back of Aidan's head."

"Jesus Christ?" I said. "Where's Aidan? Is he OK?"

"He's in the bathroom," she said. "He isn't hurt."

"Why didn't you call the police?"

"We wanted to wait for you," Jamie said. "He said we shouldn't call the cops."

"Where have you been?" Sarah said. "A minute ago someone called and hung up. It could have been him."

I didn't answer her and listened to Jamie's story.

She said a man with a stocking over his head had been waiting for them on the floor of the backseat when they got in their car outside the Armada. He'd reached a hand around her mouth and held a gun to Aidan's head. If they kept quiet and followed his orders, he promised he wouldn't hurt them. He told Aidan to drive to the harbor park. When they got there, he gave Jamie an orange and white paisley hankie and said she should give it to her father. Then he left.

She went to the coffee table and picked up the hankie and handed it to me. I closed my hand around it.

Sarah was quiet, fuming.

"What's wrong, Dad? Are you in trouble?"

There was dried blood on the hankie and I put it in my pocket. I didn't want them to see it anymore.

Aidan walked in. When he saw me, I thought he was going to break down.

"Are you OK?" I said.

"Sure, Mr. Caruso." He held his breath. He was trying hard to be steady.

"We're going to call Jared," I said

Sarah stopped me and said, "I want to know what's happening."

Jamie looked ready to become a referee if Sarah's voice grew angrier.

"He's probably queer," Aidan said.

"What?" Sarah asked.

"The hankie, I think it's a gay sign. They wear them sticking out of their back pockets," he said.

I don't know where to begin.

"It's about the bathhouse murder, isn't it?" Sarah asked.

"What bathhouse murder?" Jamie wanted to know.

I didn't want to make them more terrified. I thought, *What's most important now? The cop's outside. It's late and they need sleep. They're OK. I'll wait until tomorrow and find a way to tell them almost everything.*

I considered the killer. *He's counting on me to make mistakes. He wants me to hurt them.*

I told everyone to sit down and let me call Jared.

I tried the station. He wasn't there. No answer on his

cell. I called the pager and punched in our number.

Sarah's anger was escalating. "I want to know what's going on *now*."

"Dad's trying to figure it out," Jamie said. "Don't start an argument. I can't take that."

Sarah was silent, but she narrowed her eyes to show she didn't trust me. Jamie saw it too.

"What do you remember about the guy?" I asked.

"I told you he had a stocking over his head. His face looked flattened," Jamie said.

"What about his clothes, height, age—anything?" I asked. "When Jared calls, he'll want to know. Try to remember everything."

Aidan said: "He was about six feet, with dark clothes, black pants, a black flight jacket. I looked in the rearview, but it was too dark to see much of him at first. Farther away he paused near a streetlight and I saw red block letters on the back of his jacket: DEFIANCE ENGINE 5. He walked slowly. He wasn't nervous."

He made sure they'd notice the jacket.

"I'm afraid," Jamie said. She wasn't shaking anymore, but her eyes filled up. "I don't want him to hurt you."

"It's OK," Aidan said, pulling her close.

Why haven't I taken her in my arms? What kind of comfort am I?

The phone rang. It was Jared.

"You OK?" he asked.

I told him everything. He said he'd talk to Jamie and Aidan tomorrow. He said the cop outside the house wasn't going to let anything else happen. He wanted to know whether the killer had contacted me again and when I told him I hadn't checked my messages, he said he'd be home and wanted me to call if there was any word. He said, for now, the killer's probably satisfied with the level of terror he's ratcheted up.

"He's succeeding," I said.

"Let him think so. He's going to contact you soon, and I've got a reaction he won't expect."

"A reaction?"

"We'll talk about it tomorrow. Now you settle down and calm your family, too."

I asked him if he wanted me to give the hankie to the cop outside.

"Keep it," he said. "Put it in a freezer bag. I'll get it tomorrow."

"Did you find the kid from Prospect Park?"

"He hasn't turned up anywhere. That's good news."

"I guess."

Before hanging up, he said, "I'm sorry your daughter's been drawn into this."

All the time Sarah had been putting together details. She'd already made the connection to the bathhouse. She gave me a look that meant she didn't want to hurt Jamie anymore that night. But later upstairs, when I would tell her everything, the hints of betrayal she'd ignored for so long would hit her.

Finally, I said, "No one's getting hurt. The police will find this guy."

They weren't consoled.

"It's nearly 4 in the morning. Aidan, you're staying here," I said.

"I better leave. My mother will be looking for me when she wakes up. Besides, I want to go home."

Jamie looked surprised.

"I'll take you," I said.

"No, you won't," Sarah said. "Let a police officer do it."

I called the station, and in a few minute an officer in his late twenties knocked on the door.

"I'm Patrolman Lambert. I'm here to take the boy home."

For a second, Aidan seemed to study him as if the cop were familiar. Then I realized he was still stunned by everything. He turned and kissed Jamie and said he'd see her tomorrow.

After they left, we returned to the family room. Jamie sat on the couch beside her mother. I was in the La-Z-Boy across from them. The silence didn't last long.

"You owe us an explanation," Sarah said. She'd never said I owed her anything.

I looked at Jamie. "I think the guy in the car was someone angry at me for my columns."

"What?" Sarah asked, instantly unconvinced.

"Why are you acting this way, Mom?" Jamie asked.

"It's OK," I said. "We're all nervous. Don't get angry with your mother."

I wanted to tell them something that would take the mystery out of the threats. I lied: "He's a fanatic who doesn't like my columns. Most of the time these guys want to scare you and it ends there. The cops think they know where to find him. Everything is going to be OK."

I didn't say, *Some psycho's been killing men I've picked up,* even though they'd discover this soon enough.

Sarah took the card from the Slaughter out of her pocket and looked at it. She saw me watching her but didn't say anything. Jamie didn't notice.

"What's the orange hankie mean?" Jamie asked. "The deal about a gay signal?"

"I don't know," I said, even though I didn't want to lie.

I got up and put my arm around her. I remembered the

college kid going down on me in the park and felt dirty, like a criminal.

"I'm sorry," I said.

"Why? What did you do?"

I didn't answer and she let the hankie thing die.

Sarah was immovable.

"So they really think they know how to find this guy?" Jamie asked.

"They think they're close."

For Jamie's sake, Sarah didn't challenge me.

"Does anybody know what time it is?" I asked.

"Does anybody care," Jamie sang, half-heartedly. She tightened her lips, the thing she did when she was nervous.

"Let's get some sleep, and we'll talk in the morning," I said.

"What did you do to this guy?" Jamie asked.

"I don't know," I said. "I don't know."

"Let's go upstairs, Jamie." Sarah pulled her from the couch and, wrapping an arm around her waist, they walked upstairs.

Jamie didn't kiss me.

"Try to get some sleep. I want to check something on the computer before I turn in."

They were silent as I watched them turn down the upstairs hallway.

On my way to the study I saw the unmarked car outside. He'd turned his engine on and white exhaust streamed into the night.

At my desk, I clicked on my mail server and waited for messages. I thought of Buddy's letter about the parking patrol. He'd said that they were all fags. Maybe Winchel wasn't the killer. Maybe Buddy followed me to Seattle and discovered me at the Slaughter. Maybe it really was a reader, someone who'd tracked me to the bathhouse. I thought, *Whoever killed him put his fucking hand around my daughter's mouth.* I winced at the picture of it in my mind. *That hand packed the penis into the box, too.* Would he do all of this because he hated fags? I thought about calling Jared, but didn't.

There were no new messages. On the desk beside the computer was a Styrofoam pellet with a light reddish stain. I picked it up and decided to toss it into the sewer grate, but remembered the cruiser parked by the curb. Between my fingers, the slimy Styrofoam felt almost fleshy. I went to the bathroom and dropped it in the toilet bowl. When I flushed and fresh water returned, it shot back up, bobbed and floated to the center.

"Jesus," I said. "How am I going to stop him?"

I flushed a second time, and when water rushed back in, the pellet was gone.

Sarah was sitting up when I entered the bedroom. She leaned against the headboard and looked at me. The card from the Slaughter was on the nightstand beside her.

"I want to know what's going on," she said.

"It's the hardest thing I've ever had to explain." I sat on the edge of the bed, and inadvertently, I slid my hand under her thigh.

"You were at the bathhouse earlier," she said.

"I think I met the guy who was killed there."

"You weren't working on a story."

"I lied about that."

She swatted my hand away and said, "Jesus, Dan. I don't know you."

I could tell she was doing everything possible not to hate me.

"Why don't you say it?" she asked.

"I'm trying to."

"The Slaughter isn't a steakhouse."

"It's a gay bar. I met someone there on Thursday night, and everything started the next day."

"Everything?" she asked and fell silent for a while before she continued. "How long have you been fucking men—and afterward climbing into bed with me?"

Before I could say anything, she winced and said, "Jesus, AIDS."

I couldn't tell her about Stephen Hart and the bottle of AZT in the desk drawer.

"I didn't do anything that would have put you at risk that way."

"Isn't *that* selfless," she said. Then she looked at me intently. With uncharacteristic sarcasm she said, "You mean you haven't fucked me for years because you didn't want to give me AIDS."

I couldn't say anything.

"You're involved in the murder at the bathhouse?"

"I think the guy there was killed because of me, but I don't know why."

She was silent a while and asked, "How long?"

"What?"

"How long have you been fucking men?" Her anger was palpable.

"Not now, Sarah. Don't do this now."

"Don't tell me what to do."

"I'm sorry."

"That's never been enough, though I always let you say it. I'm sick of it."

"I know."

"You don't know a goddamn thing. How long?"

"Please. Don't do this."

Then she had a revelation. Something she'd sensed for hours, but the enormity of it struck her for the first time.

"What happened to Jamie in that car involves your fucking secret life. And you say you're *sorry.*"

"The police are outside. We're going to be OK."

"Get out." Her voice was empty as a windless night, the kind of night no one would want to die in, absolutely still, with no hint of redemption anywhere.

easter sunday

The patrolman parked outside wouldn't let me leave.

"Detective O'Connor wants the house zipped," said the officer. He was young, maybe 23, tops.

I wanted to go down to the newspaper to see whether Buddy had e-mailed me there and then read through his old letters, the ones I'd kept. I wanted to do something that would help me understand what I had to do to stop him.

"I'm driving down to the *Record*," I said.

"No, you're not." He didn't hesitate.

"I have to check some things out on the computer. I'm going."

"You're staying. That's the order from downtown." He inched his cruiser about five feet forward to block the driveway. "If you want, we can call O'Connor. But it's late. I advise against it."

The patrolman told me his name—Italian—but I forgot it almost immediately. He looked Italian, his face darkened with a sandy shadow even though he'd probably shaved that morning, brown eyes, a slightly Roman nose between strong cheekbones. I wondered how much he knew. He probably understood this had something to do with the bathhouse murder. Was he thinking, *Where does this fag think he's going now?*

"You know it's Easter," he said, shifting gears. "I bet my kid is up looking for candy before I get home."

I thought about the man carrying a white-chocolate bunny across the street while I was out hunting.

"You've got a kid," I said. "You look too young to have a kid."

"His name's Anthony. He's almost four. I look younger than I am."

"I've got a daughter."

"I know."

"You don't love anything more, ever, than your child."

"I know."

It was almost 4 in the morning, and I'd only slept a few hours since I woke up in the firefighter's empty bed on Friday.

"Maybe I won't go to the newspaper," I said. "Maybe I'll just try to find what I need on my computer in the study."

"That's a good idea, Mr. Caruso. Your family wouldn't want to wake up and find that you're not there."

He took a thermos from a bag. A long, sleek one, modern, the kind Starbucks sells.

"My wife made some coffee—still hot. Want a swig? It's mocha java—Ocean Roasters, good stuff."

"No, thanks." I thought about going inside for a whiskey, but I didn't have a taste for it. I didn't want a drink. I wanted to make sure I knew exactly what I was doing.

"Sometimes it's good to talk about things after a crime happens." He poured coffee into the thermos cap, not much bigger than a shot glass. "Just a little bit, every hour or so, keeps me alert."

The air between his window and me filled with the thick scent of mocha java.

"Maybe I'll have one," I said.

The coffee tasted fine, and I was relieved that he'd distracted me from a situation that was going to get a lot worse.

I remembered his comment about Easter and asked, "What do you think of the resurrection?"

What if I'd said, "What do you think of an erection?" I didn't want my thinking going that way, and couldn't believe I'd let it after all that had happened. Even so, I stood at the curb before him and thought: *He's handsome.* This time I knew I wasn't going anywhere with it.

It was a while before he answered. He wasn't caught off guard by the question, but he was thinking. I could tell by the way the muscles around his eyes tightened.

"I used to believe in all of it," he said. "The Father, Son, and Holy Ghost, the crucifix, the wine and bread, the hosannas. I was an altar boy, six years. But to tell you the truth, lately, after what I've seen, I don't think about religion too much. Maybe it's not the thing to say on Easter, and I suppose, if anything, I'm superstitious. But since you asked, how about you, Mr. Caruso?"

"Either it happened or it didn't. No way of proving it one way or the other."

"I'll buy that," he said.

He surprised me and asked: "So you think this killer's stalking you?"

I didn't know whether I should be talking to him, but I was relieved to have the chance and said, "He's threatening me and my family. He wants something. Jared thinks he's going to slip up soon."

"Detective O'Connor knows what he's doing. He's smart. If he's in your corner, you won't get hurt."

"Right."

"This killer seems smart—a dissembler. I heard O'Connor talking to Lambert about him. He's a challenge. But O'Connor's at his best when the challenge is tough."

"Right." It was clear the cop was trying to boost my spirits. I thought about his word, *dissembler.* It described me too. An adulterer. A father who squandered my daughter's respect because I lacked the courage to tell her the truth.

The cop sensed I was losing focus and said, "You look tired. Why don't you go in and get some sleep before the sun comes up."

I thought again about the resurrection and said, "It's the unexpected act of kindness that amazes me. I'll take it any day over the resurrection."

He nodded and said, "Like the bumper sticker."

"What bumper sticker?"

"The 'random act of kindness' one. My wife put one on her car." He paused and said, "You look really tired."

"I am."

"You'll feel better after some sleep. It's always better the day or so after you've been scared. Don't worry." He reached out of the open window and patted my arm.

His hand on my arm felt like a blessing.

"Night, Mr. Caruso."

I waved without saying a word.

■

I went back in, careful not to make any noise when I closed the door. All of the lights were still lit. I slipped off my shoes and walked upstairs to make sure everyone was

OK. I shut the light in the bathroom. I went to the doorway of my daughter's room and stood there a while, as I'd done hundreds of times before. Miraculously, she was sleeping. She was still wearing jeans and a T-shirt she bought at the zoo. Her shoes—thick-heeled, black leather ones, more like a workman's than a girl's—were on the floor at the foot of the bed. I felt regret so black that I thought I'd never feel anything else again. She was lying on her side. I bent down to kiss her. Her lips were still pursed. I was afraid I'd never kiss her again.

I shut the light. On the way to my bedroom I thought about the policeman in the cruiser. He'd see the lights go out one by one and think, *Good, they're trying to rest.* I hoped he'd never know a loss as cavernous as this.

At the door of our bedroom, I whispered, "Sarah."

She didn't answer. I didn't know whether she was asleep or ignoring me. Before tonight, when she slept I used to imagine she found a satisfaction in the dark that I never could achieve. It was almost unbearably beautiful to see her wrapped in her dreams. Sometimes I'd rest against the brass bars of the headboard—a voyeur—with no claim to a share of her peace. I loved her more than I'd ever shown, more than I could explain now that she was drawn into this. I always knew, though, that I would never love her the way a husband must love his wife if he isn't going to hurt her someday. Whenever we fucked, I dreamed of naked men.

I turned off the light and waited. No movement, not the slightest rustle of the sheets. *Good,* I thought, *maybe she's asleep.*

Downstairs, at the bottom of the stairway, I flipped off the hallway lights. Room after room darkened: kitchen, bath, the family and dining rooms. I kept the foyer lit and peeked out the door to see the policeman at his post. His window was still open. I saw a nervous flickering inside his cruiser that must have been coming from his laptop screen-saver. I considered going out and telling him to close the window because someone watching could see the fidgety computer light. But it didn't seem all that important.

I sat at my desk and thought about calling Jared but decided not to. If the murderer asked me what the cop was doing outside the house, I'd tell him the police think I know something about the bathhouse murder and that's why they're watching me. I'd say, "That's what you wanted, you bastard, isn't it?"

I thought of calling Bellemy, but it was past midnight in the West. I would tell him I was sorry about hanging up like that earlier. I'd confide in him about some of what was hap-pening and see whether he could find out what Winchel looked like. Maybe he could get me a photograph, a logo from the Port Townsend *Ledger*. I'd call him before Jared arrived tomorrow.

I heard a metallic tapping against the window pane behind me and opened the curtain. A hand was hanging on twine from a plant hook. A ring on one finger struck the glass as the hand dangled in the breeze.

"For Christ's sake, no," I said aloud.

I opened the window and looked out. No one anywhere. The hand brushed the top of my head and I reared back. There was a note pinned to it. When I tore it off, the hand fell from the hook to the ground. The note:

> For your collection. It looked sweeter with the han-kie tied to the wrist. Orange. Anything goes. Check out this site: www.friendsofdesade.darkerlove.com I'll be in touch by e-mail, later tonight or in the morning. I want to meet you, soon.

I tried Jared's cell. No answer. I tried the station and someone told me he'd gone home.

"It's 5 in the morning? You OK?" the cop said.

"Tell him I called. It's important," I said.

I tried his home and he didn't answer. I called the beeper and punched in my phone number.

I returned to the window and looked at the hand. *He's making sure I'm getting used to this.* I shined a small table lamplight on it and saw it was blotched with dried blood, the fingers bunched close to the palm. It was beginning to smell. I remembered the orange hankie in my pocket and fished it out. *This hand slid across my chest when he was going down on me.*

I typed in the Web address and wondered why Jared hadn't called back.

On my screen appeared block letters in deep red: A MEDITERRANEAN TOUR. There were thumbnails of four beautiful men. Jean Paul, an academic from Paris, "renowned for his stamina and virility." Taliba, from Morocco: "a bodybuilder and exotic dancer who enjoys working up a sweat." Gianluca, a model from Bologna: "Sweet 18, he models and paints erotica." And Spiros, "the Colossus of Rhodes, an escort and a part-time plumber, naked as ever, testing out some of his handiwork." The Jean Paul thumbnail looked a little like Stephen Hart. I clicked on the shrunken image, and in seconds the naked academic from Paris filled the screen.

His hair was cut close to his scalp, but just long enough to slide your fingers through, not so butch it was like a dome of sandpaper. Another man with a secret life. He couldn't be Stephen Hart. His chest, his thighs, his sex were different. I was breathing fast from the gathering horror.

"Click here," it said under a black bar, *"for words from my favorite writer—Marquis de Sade."*

I clicked and was sent to another photograph: Jean Paul in black leather, chains, and a mask. His cock was visible through a slit in his pants. In a box beside him, some text, presented in more deep red letters on a black background: COME AND SEE WHAT DE SADE SAYS ABOUT LOVE...SEXUAL RESTRAINT...THE AFFLICTION OF PAIN MORE BEAUTIFUL THAN ANY TENDERNESS. "What does one want when one is engaged in the sexual act? To be the object of utter attention... Every man wants to be a tyrant when he fornicates. No sensation more tyrannical in its demand for attention is keener than pain."

I thought about the cuffs in the crystal bowl in Stephen Hart's apartment. What was the murderer trying to tell me? I thought about bathhouse sex. The anonymity of it. The killer looking for prey in a blackened berth. Someone like me waiting for sex. The murderer was teaching me a lesson in control. He didn't kill because he hated gay men; he killed because he loved making others suffer. I read on: "Happiness lies only in that which excites, and the only thing that excites is crime."

The killer believed I understood the pleasure he found in murder. My own obsession with clandestine sex could make him think, *Two agents of one dark recklessness, and mine satisfies me unconditionally. Caruso will understand and envy me while he hates me.*

Sade's last words: "All creatures are born isolated and have no need of one another."

The murderer believed I shared his vision of dark Narcissus. Why wouldn't he believe this of someone like me who'd lied to everyone for so long—someone subsisting on deception. I stared at Jean Paul's nakedness and felt criminal.

There was a scraping sound like sandpaper below the windowsill and, for a moment, I thought the hand had come alive. I looked and saw Chelsea. She'd been scratching at it with one paw, and when she saw me at the window, she snatched it and ran into the woods. I mouthed, "Chelsea, no," actually too astonished to raise my voice in protest.

Then I heard footsteps nearby. They were coming from the foyer. When I looked up, my daughter was at the doorway.

"I'm scared," she said.

I managed to walk back to the desk and clicked the de Sade file closed before she reached me. She kissed me on my shoulder.

"Hold me," she said.

I put my arms around her and felt her tears on my neck. *The hand—the cops can find it later. I can't do anything about it now.*

I held her silently for a long time. She tucked her head below my shoulder, like a nesting sparrow.

Finally, I said, "It's OK, Jamie."

"It's not OK, Dad. Nothing's OK." She was still weepy. "I woke up and thought about his hand around my mouth."

Jesus.

"I know," I said and held her closer.

"I could taste it. It was sour, like metal. I thought about biting it and then running, but he had the gun pointed at Aidan's head."

Like metal, I thought. *Remains of dried blood from the bathhouse murder. That's what she'd tasted.*

"You did everything right, kiddo. What's most important is that you're safe. You and Aidan are OK."

"He let us go."

Jamie sounded as if she was speaking about a dream, as if she were walking underwater. She hadn't slept more than an hour. I held her tight and hated myself for all the terror I'd caused her.

"Why did he want you to have the hankie?" she asked.

"I don't know. He must think I'd understand. I haven't been able to figure it out." I didn't want to lie, but I couldn't tell her. I hoped I'd never have to.

"He said you'd know. He didn't sound crazy. He wasn't nervous. He was patient, his voice was even gentle." She'd stopped crying.

"Jamie, try not to think about him anymore tonight. He's not going to hurt us."

"Why is the window wide open?" she asked. She looked down at the note on the stand.

"That dog prowls around at night like a cat," I said. "Chelsea was digging in the grass there a few minutes ago.

I picked up the note and slipped it in my pocket.

"What were you doing on the computer?" she asked.

"Checking e-mails."

"Did he contact you?"

"No." The intensity of her interest worried me. *He's expecting this. He's hoping terror will consume us. He's glad my helplessness will make me hate him.*

"What's his name again?"

"Buddy. He calls himself Buddy."

"That's sick, At least he could have a real name. Why did he single you out?"

"He started writing to me a long time ago about my columns. At first his comments were just bizarre, but they become more threatening. I can't figure out why he's doing this."

"Did he kill the guy in the bathhouse?"

I didn't answer and could tell she understood my silence meant that he probably did.

"Mom thinks you know *too much* about the bath-house murder and had something to do with it. What does she mean?"

"I'm not sure. There've been some targeted killings in the city, but Buddy may not be involved. But maybe he was—that's what the police are trying to find out."

"Targeted? You mean gay murders."

I nodded and could tell she was going somewhere, and all I could do was wait for what she was going to say next.

"You're gay," she said.

Her words were like a door swinging open. Surprised by how easy it was, I said, "That's right, I'm gay."

"I think I knew last year. We were in Key West. The thought crossed my mind when we went by a shop with a bunch of gay sex toys and calendars in the window. I saw the way you looked at them. I never said anything. Mom doesn't see these things."

I took her arm and smiled nervously. We walked over to the couch and sat down.

She said, "It's OK, Dad. I still love you."

She hugged me and didn't know what else to say.

I searched my memory for a lyric, a phrase, something that could show her I was grateful for what she had just done. I searched for any stray line that might make her laugh: *The cake is melting in the rain.* Senseless. *Show me the way to the next whiskey bar.* Don't go there. *Everybody's got something to hide except for me and my monkey.* Too easy. It didn't matter, though, because she wasn't in the mood for the game.

"You won't lie to me anymore," she said. "You're not lying to me about Buddy, the guy tonight."

"The murder in the bathhouse had something to do with me, but I'm not sure what. I can't tell you everything right now. I won't lie, but I just can't share all I know. Trust me, please."

"Aidan said he thought gays are sick. We had a fight about it the other day. God, he'll never change his mind after this."

I think I heard her laugh, a low astonishing one, much older than her age.

"He's got time to learn," I said. "A lot of young guys don't understand."

"He's not perfect."

"Who is?"

"I want to hear some Maura O'Connell. The song about crazy dreams."

How am I going to protect her?

The phone rang. It was Jared.

"Wait a second," I told him.

I put in the CD and said I had to talk to him and I'd be back soon. She rested her head on a pillow. I saw her eyes close. I walked into the hallway and leaned against the door-frame.

"Jared," I said.

"Are you OK?"

"He sent another souvenir."

"The hand?"

"That's right."

"What did you do with it?"

"It was hanging from a hook outside my study and fell to the ground when I reached for a note pinned to it. You won't believe it, but a dog grabbed it and carried it into the woods."

"What dog?"

"Chelsea. The neighbor's border collie."

"Fuck this shit, Dan. I'll send another cop over. Where's the woods?"

"In back of the house."

"What's the dog look like?"

"Black with white markings on her chest, like any border collie."

He got on the other phone and dispatched someone.

When he came back on, he said, "Look out the window and see if you see that fuckin' dog anywhere."

I stepped back into the room and looked out the window. "No dog," I whispered.

"Can't you speak louder?"

"Jamie's asleep right here. I don't want her to see any of this."

"Is the cop there yet?"

"No." I thought a moment, and said, "If the killer's watching, we don't want him to see this activity. We don't want him to think I called the cops about the hand."

"We want that hand," he said.

"OK." I was so confused I would have said OK to anything.

I saw the cop walking past the window: Lambert, who'd taken Aidan home earlier.

"He's here," I said.

"Good."

Then I saw Chelsea. She was back by the window, and Lambert was standing still about 20 feet behind. She sat and looked at me, the hand dangling by a finger from her mouth. I put down the phone.

"Stay, Chelsea," I said.

Lambert didn't want to spook her.

"Mr. Caruso," he said. "Keep the dog's attention."

He inched forward, but it was clear Chelsea wasn't going anywhere. She'd fetched it back and wanted someone to take it from her. She didn't care—me or the cop, she wanted to play.

Before I could say I thought she'd let him take it, he rushed the dog and pinned her. I heard her whimper. He grabbed the hand from her mouth, and as soon as he rose, she bolted home.

He gave me a look that said, *How ridiculous is this?* He dropped the hand into an evidence bag and left for his cruiser.

I heard Jared on the phone: "What the fuck is going on?"

"It's over. The cop's got the hand."

"Christ, what next?" he said.

I looked over at Jamie. She shifted on the couch but didn't wake up.

Back in the hallway, I said, "Jared, there was a note. It sent me to some porn Web site with writings by the Marquis de Sade. He said he'd reach me by e-mail today. He said he wanted to meet me soon."

"Where is it?"

"What?"

"The note. Did you give it to Lambert?"

"I have it."

I didn't tell him about the naked French academic who looked a little like the firefighter. That had to be a coincidence.

He sounded calmer.

"I figured he'd want to meet you—it's part of the cat-and-mouse he's playing, but he won't know about our trap," Jared said.

"What trap?"

"We're working on something. I'll discuss it with you later. Just remember, if you talk to him, make sure he doesn't know you've said anything to the cops about him. If he asks about the unmarked outside, your conversations with me, you tell him you think you're a suspect. You're being watched and questioned because we think you're involved. That's what he wants. Let's make sure he's convinced. Let's hope we had some luck and he didn't see Lambert and the fuckin' dog. After all, it's almost 6 in the morning. He's got to sleep, too."

"Do you think he's the reporter from Seattle?"

"Maybe."

"Enger have any more information?"

"We haven't talked since Saturday afternoon before the bathhouse murder. He's flying in late Monday. I hope this will be over by then."

"Over?"

"If we get lucky."

I looked in on Jamie. She was still sleeping.

"Enger thinks I'm the prime suspect?" I asked.

"Let him think so. He'll discover he's wrong soon enough."

"I'll tell Bellemy to find a photograph of Winchel."

"Christ, I didn't think of that. But I found out Winchel might not be in Washington. He wasn't at the newspaper on Friday, one of his scheduled days off, no answer at his home. No one at the paper knows where he might be, but that's not unusual because they said he's a loner. He could be the bastard, and for all we know, he's in town. I should have gotten a photograph. Keep thinking. See how useful you can be."

"Why didn't Enger say anything about Winchel?"

"Maybe he's playing this close to his vest too."

"But shouldn't you be sharing everything you know?"

"Look, cops get territorial in a case that crosses borders like this. Maybe he thinks you're the primary and doesn't want to give me a reason to take the pressure off you here. Cops are suspicious. He won't decide how much he wants to share until he meets me. It's no surprise."

"If I'd met Winchel at the conference, you'd think I might have recognized him since then."

"These guys know how to hide."

"You think he hates gays?"

"Usually, there's more than hate driving a serial. One thing's for sure, he is crazy smart. But these guys trip up and this one's time is closing in. You're going to help us smoke him out. I don't have all the details nailed down. Everything depends on how we catch him."

Smoke him out, details nailed down—the cop clichés confused me. *Crazy smart: Now that makes sense,* I thought.

"I'm worried: Sarah and Jamie can't be put in any more jeopardy," I said.

"They won't be."

I wasn't convinced and said, "I've already fucked up their lives. I want to be sure he doesn't hurt them."

"He won't. By the way, happy Easter."

I didn't say anything.

"Dan," he said. "You're going to be OK. Your family is going to be OK."

Easter, I thought.

"What does Easter have to do with anything?" I asked, noticeably irritated.

"I just wanted to distract you. You're too tense. You know, Easter: It's a time of redemption. Hope."

I was silent for a while and then said: "What about the FBI? They're involved because he's crossed state lines. Maybe they can help?"

"The more cops in this, the more likely he'll decide to go underground. We want to keep him out there. I control the chain of evidence in Providence. We can manage this guy without him catching on."

I remembered the college kid. "What about the kid in the park?"

"No reports of another victim, and since you haven't received a souvenir, I think he might have slipped by. I hope he's your last lover boy for a while."

"He wasn't my lover boy."

"OK, your trick. No more tricks."

I remembered Stephen Hart entering me. *Another trick,* I thought. *When the firefighter knew he was going to die and while he was breathing his last breaths, he didn't think of me. So why is any of this happening? I didn't mean anything to him. Why kill any of them? They were all just tricks.*

"You should have told me about Seattle yesterday afternoon," Jared said. "For a while, that omission made me pause, and I thought, *Maybe he isn't just a victim here.* You've got to know what it looks like when someone in a mess like you're in withholds information like this. I'm not Scotland Yard. I'm your friend."

"He told me I shouldn't bring in the cops. I was afraid he'd hurt my family. Maybe I was wrong."

Jared had stopped listening and said: "What I don't understand is what made you so fucking horny? First this guy in Seattle; two days later you visit a bathhouse; that same night you're cruising on Prospect Terrace like you're on some suicide mission."

I don't understand, so why should he? He doesn't even know about the guy in the stall at O'Hare. Jesus, is he dead, too?

"Any word about a murder in O'Hare on Friday night?" I asked.

"Another trick?"

"You haven't heard anything about a stiff in Chicago with a condom pinned to his chest."

"No."

"You would have heard something if it happened?"

"If some stiff anywhere is discovered with a condom pinned on him, that's right, I'd know."

I thought, *Why is he helping me if he thinks I'm scum?*

"I don't understand why you're taking these risks," I said.

"I told you it's my job. And you're a friend. That always complicates a cop's job."

Before I could utter something stupid, he said, "I want to talk to you later about what *we* can do. Like I said, maybe we'll get lucky, maybe we'll even catch him dead."

What he said didn't register at first because I was thinking about the night outside the warehouse. Then I thought, *If we catch him dead, Stephen Hart, the bathhouse trick— maybe no one will link them to me. But he's a cop, how can he be thinking this? Cops want to catch murderers alive; cops don't set out to kill the perps.*

"You mean we'd be running on a separate track?"

"Not exactly. There would always be backup here and some cops who know more than others, but if *we* bring him in dead, we'd save a lot of trouble for everyone."

"You can't withhold information like this. This doesn't make sense."

Then he told me something that astonished me. He said his father had left home when he was two years old. About a year ago he showed up out of the blue. They had coffee at Fellini's. A week later, dinner. He was a mailman in New London, moved there from Houston about a year before. He'd been in Vietnam. He'd been on drugs and alcohol most of his life until he got clean and, after a lot of bottle-washer jobs, ended up in the postal service. He'd returned because he hoped to get to know his son. Jared said that after a couple of meetings, he decided he didn't want his father to walk back into his life so easily. He refused to see him, and then, one night when he was patrolling downcity, he discovered him talking to someone outside the Yukon. He saw his dad put a hand down the man's pants and kiss the guy. Later that night, he was dispatched to Kennedy Plaza: report of a stiff next to the skating rink. He found his father dead, one knife wound in the heart.

"Christ," I said. "I'm sorry."

"I'm sorry he's dead, but part of me feels he was just a stranger. And part of me feels I should have hauled his ass out of the alley next to the Yukon. I knew about the dangers."

"So you think the maniac killed your father too?"

"Maybe, but it wasn't the same M.O."

"Your father's not part of the investigation?"

"I didn't tell anyone what I saw outside the Yukon. No one knows he was my dad."

"That doesn't make sense."

"Maybe you're right. But this bastard probably didn't kill him. It happened a year before the serial's first hit. Like I said, different M.O. And what the fuck does my father have to do with you? He wasn't one of your tricks. But maybe you're right. Maybe killing this guy is kind of personal."

I didn't know what to say.

"Your guy hates queers, but that's just the beginning. What's driving him is that he loves killing. We're going to find him. Maybe we can do it before too many cops scare him into a black hole. Remember what he said about your family. He means it."

Jesus, we're thinking of killing him on our own.

"Look, it's nearly 5. Get some sleep. You've got a lot to tell your family. Just make sure you don't say anything about this thing. And when he contacts you, make sure you call me right away. That's crucial. Understand?"

"OK." *This thing? What was I doing?*

"Sleep," he said, and hung up.

I wished I'd told him why the firefighter wasn't just a trick. I wanted to tell him I loved his arm around my shoulder in the park. Then I remembered the AZT in the desk drawer and thought, *I've still got to deal with* that *fear. I'll get a test sometime next week. It will be negative. I won't be ravaged by AIDS.* I thought about my father. I wanted to touch Jared's arm and tell him he cared more about his father than he knew. Maybe Jared cared more about me than he knew.

I slid down the wall and sat on the hallway floor and wondered how I was going to manage. Framed reproductions of MGM musicals surrounded me and everything seemed absurd. In a Hollywood mood, my wife put up the gay icons—unwittingly: Judy Garland hiking through the woods with the Scarecrow, Tin Man and Cowardly Lion. Gene Kelly, Debbie Reynolds and Donald O'Connor dressed in yellow raincoats and carrying umbrellas. Reynolds, my wife's favorite, as the unsinkable Molly Brown barely escaping a falling statue in the ballroom of a doomed ship.

I heard Maura O'Connell still singing in the study and remembered Jamie was sleeping on the couch. I returned and sat beside her, careful not to wake her. I stretched out and put my arm around her. O'Connell's voice was soothing. I thought about Sarah alone upstairs and wondered whether I should wake her and ask her to come down. I touched Jamie's hair and thought, *What did de Sade know about tenderness?* I never wanted anyone to be hurt. The music almost soothed me—a song about the Isle of Malachy. But she sang about the sea gone dry.

I drifted off about halfway through "Just in Time" with

137

Jamie sound asleep beside me. Like this we rested, without the hint of a nightmare anywhere.

■

I heard my wife banging pans in the kitchen. She was cooking breakfast. I smelled bacon frying, coffee brewing. My daughter was gone. There were footsteps in the hall. *Jamie*, I thought. *She'll sit and talk with Sarah about how afraid she is. Sarah's thinking how she hates me for bringing this home.*

I pictured the murderer's hand over my daughter's mouth and thought, *He won't stop there.* I pictured the mutilated corpses.

Sarah walked in and poked me in the shoulder and said there was a call.

"It's Bellemy," she said.

I barely heard. She held the portable phone in her hand like a hammer, and in that middle ground before daylight captures a sleeper's attention, I thought, *She's going to crack open my skull.* I'd concocted the revenge for my own benefit, an imagined payback to help settle the score for what I'd done. A dream of restitution. Fat chance.

She poked me again. "It's the reporter from Washington."

She handed me the phone and sat at the other end of the couch. When I rose and left the room, she followed me with slow eyes. I turned into the bathroom and shut the door.

"Bellemy," I said. "I'm sorry about yesterday. There's a lot to tell you. But most of it is going to have to wait."

"I'm flying out there with Enger" he said. "I shouldn't be talking to you, but I am because I don't think you're the killer."

"Thanks."

"I've known you a long time, and I've always sensed you were keeping lots of secrets. One of them I've guessed."

"OK."

"You screwed Stephen Hart."

I didn't say anything.

After a while, he said, "Enger knows, too. At first he thought you were the chief suspect. Now he's thinking it's probably Winchel. Jealousy. The guy's disappeared. He could be in Providence."

I didn't tell him about the bathhouse murder, though he'd read about it online soon enough. He'd wonder again why I had so much to hide.

"I can't talk now. There are some family matters going on."

"No shit."

"Then I'm going to meet the cops later to discuss everything. I'm hoping, though, you'll do me a favor. Find a photo of Winchel, a thumbnail from the *Port Townsend Ledger*. Maybe Enger has one. E-mail it to me before you leave."

"You're not blowing me off."

I wondered whether he considered the implications of what he'd said.

"No. You'll get the whole story."

"I'll find the mug."

"Thanks."

I said goodbye and sat on the toilet seat. I closed my eyes and saw myself throwing Stephen's penis into the sea.

I could go into the kitchen and explain as much as they could handle. Or I could wait a while longer, let them have some time together. I heard rustling below the window. It was the dog. I opened the window and said, "Chelsea, get the fuck out of here."

I returned to the study and checked messages. It was waiting, sent at 8:04, while Jamie and I were sleeping nearby on the couch. The sender line: "Excited yet? Yours only."

Recognize the orange hankie, chum? I love the sloppy seconds you leave. I like it better when you break them in for me. Who's next?

I like that preppy with your daughter outside the Armada last night. Maybe you can get him alone sometime, invite him for a father-to-daughter's-boyfriend talk. Go down on him. I'll handle it from there. I couldn't find your Prospect Terrace trick, the one with the knife. Nasty boy. But I'll keep my eyes peeled. Maybe one night on a hunt he'll choose me like he did you.

I want to meet you tonight, and if you don't show up I can't promise your family will be safe for very long. By the way, I know the cops think you're involved. You're thinking, *He's fucking omniscient*, and you're right.

Meet me tonight in New York City. There's a place on 10th Avenue and 13th Street, the meat-packing district, maybe you know it already. If you do, your education is more advanced than I believed. It's called the Lure.

It's mask night. You have to wear a mask to get in. No Halloween disguise. Just a plain mask. A black leather one. A hood would be nice, like a condemned man might wear.

And don't tell your friend the detective about this. If you do I promise I'll be angry and I'll take it out on your home sweet home.

I'll know you even in a mask. I'll know you by your eyes. I'll know your ass. Don't leave before midnight because you don't want to miss me. Maybe before we talk, you'll meet someone special, someone you'll break in for me. No fems, please. I don't like fems. By the way, you can call me 'Yours.' Yours only.

I looked for the return address: Sixthman@javanet-cafe.net. He'd sent it from a public cafe. Maybe he's already in New York. No hint at all he might be Winchel. Nothing about the firefighter. *"Don't tell your friend the detective."*

I picked up the phone to call Jared and clicked off before it rang. *If I don't do what he says, he'll kill them for sure.*

I printed out the message and deleted it and hoped the techs coming that afternoon wouldn't discover it. I knew what I was doing was crazy, but I didn't think I had another choice.

I searched for flights leaving that morning for Tampa. The next was at 11:50. I booked two e-tickets that they could pick up at check-in. *They'll be safer at Sarah's parents' if something goes wrong.* It was almost 10. Soon I'd be on the train.

In the kitchen, my wife and daughter were staring at a photograph on the counter. Fried eggs and bacon were growing dry and leathery on the stove. The counter was cleared except for a bowl of bananas and oranges and the photograph and a white envelope near the fruit. They looked at me—speechless.

"What?" I asked.

They couldn't talk. All of their effort was directed at capturing enough air to breathe. The life they knew had collapsed under them, dropping them into a slow free fall.

I picked up the photograph. The kid was on his knees below the statue of Roger Williams on Prospect Terrace. My pants and boxers were gathered around my ankles. His head was drawn far enough back from my crotch to show my cock in his mouth. My head arced back against the stone pedestal. My expression was frozen in grotesque rapture.

My humiliation was complete. I felt numb, empty, soulless. I wasn't in the same speechless free fall that had swept away Sarah and Jamie; for these seconds I didn't exist.

"I'm sorry," I said.

Jamie turned away and hid her face in Sarah's shoulders. She couldn't look anymore.

"I don't know how I can ever explain. I need to explain so much before I can try to talk about this."

"Don't," Sarah said.

"Where did you get it?" I asked.

Jamie lifted her head. "It was taped to the window on the kitchen door."

She picked up the envelope and handed it to me. On the front was printed: "For Jamie. From a chum of your dad." And below it was written: "A picture, a thousand words."

They've got to catch that flight.

Sarah said, "We're all in danger because of you."

Did he leave it there when he tied up the hand? Why didn't the cop outside see him? Maybe he left it when the cop was talking to me? Why didn't we notice? He was back here in the morning. If I didn't follow his orders, he'd hurt them. He'd kill them. I didn't have a choice. *"Don't tell your friend the detective."*

"Who is he, Dad?" Jamie asked.

"I don't know. I'm going to find out."

"What about calling the detective, your friend Jared? He should know what's going on."

Sarah remained strangely silent.

"First, I need to do something on my own."

Jamie looked even more frightened. I retrieved the flight information and gave it to Sarah, but she threw it on the table and hit me. First a slap across my face. Then she punched me with her fists, hammered them against my chest. Jamie tried to pull her away, but she fought to batter me as hard as she could. Finally, she dropped into a kitchen chair and covered her eyes. If she was crying, I couldn't hear.

Jamie tried to comfort her. "It's OK. We'll figure this out. Don't hate him," she said.

Her sympathy was devastating. She turned to me as if she wanted to believe I could explain everything.

I pulled Sarah's hands from her face, and said, "Pay attention. You have to leave. You have to get to the airport, get the next flight to Tampa. I'll call you at your mother's later this evening. Don't even pack, just go."

I picked up the flight information and put it in her hand more forcefully than I'd intended. I looked outside and saw the unmarked car still there. I picked up the photo and thought about the kid. It could help the police find him.

I said, "When I'm gone, you give this photograph to the cop outside and tell him to make sure Jared gets it. Tell the cop to take you to the airport, and if he gives you any trouble, call Jared and he'll make sure you get to the flight. It leaves just before noon. You have to go—*now*."

"You're destroying us," she said.

"This isn't about us. That's what we'll have to deal with later. Do what I say. If you don't, he'll kill you. He'll kill Jamie, too."

They were stunned.

"What's going on?" Jamie asked.

"Just make sure you're on that plane," I said.

I walked out the kitchen door and leapt the fence into a neighbor's backyard. I headed to the path in the woods that led downtown. When I turned to look back, I saw Chelsea about six feet away. She watched me with sad, nervous eyes. She didn't follow.

They'll do what I told them. They'll get the plane to Tampa and be safer there than in Providence.

the lure

I hid in one of the men's room stalls until the announcement of the *Yankee Clipper*'s arrival crackled through the train station's speakers. Some guy stood outside the door and peeked into the slit while I sat on the toilet, my pants zipped and buckled. All I could see was an eye, his mouth, two legs in jeans and sneakers, worn and dirty. When he tried to open the door, I coughed. He didn't leave. I said, "Get the fuck out of here. I'm a cop." He left like the wind.

It was 11:15. They'd be waiting to board the plane. *They're thinking about the photograph in Prospect Park. The image of me that will remain with them forever. I belong in this bathroom stall.*

I decided I would tell Jared that I didn't have a choice about meeting this maniac on my own because I didn't want him to hurt my family. I called the station and said, "This is Caruso. Is O'Connor there?"

"Where are you, Mr. Caruso? He's out looking for you.

He said it's important that you go back home." It was another detective, a woman, someone I didn't know.

"Did the cop outside the house take my wife and daughter to the airport?"

"I'm pretty sure they're on the plane," she said.

I clicked off and called home and was glad no one answered. *Good, they're on their way.* I shut off the cell so that it couldn't be traced.

I hoped I'd be on the train before Jared decided to search the station. He'd figure out I'd left to meet the murderer, but he'd think I was summoned to someplace closer: an abandoned mill in Woonsocket, a salt marsh somewhere in South County, or Glocester woods, Purgatory Chasm. He'd never guess the bastard would have picked a nightclub in Manhattan. I didn't know whether I was doing the right thing. *What if this is the final trap? He's counting on me to see him alone.* But there was no alternative; he'd made that clear by threatening my family. I felt dizzy.

The *Yankee Clipper* was on time. I looked around—not a cop anywhere. I was surprised the car wasn't crowded, and then I remembered it was Easter Sunday. I sat a couple rows behind two college kids in nylon parkas, the kind of Gap winter garb that bridges into the New England spring. They smiled at me when I walked by, and I noticed they were holding hands.

I looked out the window as the train crawled out of the tunnel. Sunlight filled the car, and triple-decker houses just outside of downtown wavered as the train picked up speed.

The other three passengers were alone. At the front a girl with earphones on her head bobbed to the music. A silver-haired woman nearby was doing the crossword puzzle in the Sunday *Times* magazine. I thought, *She's Sarah 20 years from now.* Another college kid a few rows ahead slept across two seats. His shoeless feet were tucked into a cushion. He wore thick gray athletic socks with red bands near the tops that ended in a gathering of dark hair above his ankles, barely visible below his pants cuffs. The hair on his head was black and shiny like a '50s rocker's. His body curled into an apostrophe.

The murderer wasn't in this car. *He's probably in New York, patiently waiting.*

I called Bellemy. If I couldn't get the photograph, he might, at the least, be able to describe the guy. I'd look for him in the Lure. Then I thought, *Mask night. I won't be able to see his face.*

No one answered, and I didn't leave a message.

We passed Kingston Station without stopping. By the time we crossed into Connecticut I was leaning against the window and watching the marshes and coves materialize as if they were emerging from thin air. I worried about finding a mask on Easter Sunday. How was I going to make him go away? I thought about killing him myself. It's what Jared said had to be done.

When I was a boy I imagined murdering enemies: Medusa or Cyclop; Nazis in polished knee-high black boots who patrolled railroad tracks in bad war movies; a thief ransacking the house while my parents were bound to chairs with ropes. I'd be hiding in the closet, the rifle cocked, waiting for the right time to blow away the terrorizing intruders' brains. No *In Cold Blood* in our home. Thanks to me, the boy savior. But until now, in my adult life, I'd never seriously thought of killing anyone. Jared said he knew as much: I didn't have the instinct for it.

There were herons and terns in the marshes. Tall grasses fanned out so thickly in some places that the edgy Atlantic was obscured—not obliterated but made slowly enigmatic. For miles along the shore the landscape shifted like this: meadows and patches of forest opened into parking lots and condominiums that vanished into coves and marshes and snatches of the ocean until the tall grasses swept everything away, leaving only a sunlit amber flourish. I wished I could have stepped out of the train in that instant, catching the motion of the grasses just right, to disappear into them forever.

We stopped for a half-hour in New Haven because of some electrical problem. No one got on or off our car. The college students were reading, the girl's head had stopped bobbing, the woman was still occupied with her puzzle, and the slumbering boy had shifted so that his feet, hanging over the armrest, stuck out into the aisle. I couldn't see him, but by the way the tips of his socks pointed upward, I guessed he must have been lying on his back. *I'll walk by him soon and see if his face is as beautiful as the rest of him.*

What the fuck am I doing?

I decided I wouldn't look at him again. I wouldn't take the chance that the killer would see me cast the slightest glance his way. I thought about the young man in Prospect Park. When I returned to Providence, I'd make sure the cops searched for him and told him about the danger he was in. I didn't care about the cash. *What was I doing on the hunt anyway? What if the kid is already dead, a body part missing and a condom pinned to his chest, a piece of him on ice waiting for me?*

The conductor walked down the aisle, checking tickets. He didn't wake up the boy or the other students. He asked whether I wanted a cup of coffee—complimentary on the holiday. I told him I was fine.

"Is it important to you?" he asked.

"What?"

"The holiday. I'm not a Christian. I always volunteer for this run. Christmas, too."

"I guess," I said. "What are you, Jewish?"

"Atheist. These days we're called free thinkers. I don't see the reason to dress it up like that."

He leaned his side against the wing of the seat across from me. It was clear he wanted to talk.

"I thought about being a priest," I said.

"What happened?"

I almost told him.

"I lost interest," I said.

"You met a girl, I bet. What do the Catholics call it, chastity?"

I laughed. "You mean celibacy."

"That's it. I never understood how the Church could survive with men taking that pledge."

"It's not really a pledge. It's a sacrifice."

"Right. Some sacrifice. Like the guys don't find ways to satisfy themselves. Like that bishop from Ireland who has a son over here and refuses to see him, or all that filthy stuff that's gone on for decades between priests and boys in Boston. It's a sacrifice like not eating. Sooner or later you eat."

I didn't answer right away. I was thinking about a life outside of the closet. Would I have loved a man and made a life with him now? Or would I have been alone like the nipple-clamp man in the smoky back room of the Slaughter? Maybe dead from Pneumocystis carinii pneumonia, Kaposi's sarcoma, dementia? *AIDS*, I thought. *I may get there anyway. AIDS is a place you go to, not a disease.*

When the conductor noticed my silence, he seemed embarrassed.

"I guess I talk too much about things strangers shouldn't get into. I'm sorry."

"It's OK." I said. "I'm not a believer anymore." I thought of one of the Monkees' lyrics: *I'm a believer, couldn't leave her, if I tried.* I wished Jamie were there so we could play our game.

"Sure I can't get you a cup of coffee?"

"Nothing, thanks."

"Enjoy the rest of your trip," he said. "If you want to sack out, go ahead, I'll wake you as soon as we pull into Penn."

"I'm not sleepy, but thanks."

He smiled and walked away, stopping to check the last passenger, the woman with the puzzle. I could hear them chatting about words, puzzle clues, as if they were old friends.

The tracks from New Haven to New York depart from the shore and pass through a suburban sprawl that looks like everywhere else in America. The train stops in Bridgeport and Stamford and Greenwich before dipping underground just out of Westchester County on its way to Pennsylvania Station. It was there in the tunnel under the earth that I decided I would kill the psychopath. It was there, listening to the reverberations of the train plowing its way through the living rock that I discovered how much I wanted to. I remembered Jared saying: *Maybe we'll catch him dead. Maybe you'll get lucky.* I didn't think about vengeance or justice, about saving my wife and daughter from him. It was a purely murderous desire, the first one I'd known, not much different, I thought, from the malice he must know before he decides to kill. And the thought of it left me surprisingly calm.

■

It was 6 o'clock when I walked out of Pennsylvania Station onto Seventh Avenue. I hailed a cab to 10th Avenue and West 13th Street. It tagged along the Hudson River, and between buildings, old warehouses being renovated into expensive lofts, I caught glimpses of the reddening sky as the sun set over New Jersey. I recalled passing through this neighborhood more than 20 years earlier—the place where sailors met hookers and men sought out sailors. First, I'd read about it in college, in an essay about Hart Crane, who, after drinking long into the night in a Bleecker Street bar, had wandered along the docks looking for a sailor to take into a nearby alley. Crane was the son of the Ohio candy maker who invented Life Savers. I wondered whether he was thinking of home or a sailor with spotless white pants gathered around the ankles when he wrote:

> *We have seen*
> *The moon in lonely alleys make*
> *a grail of laughter of an empty ash can.*

Years ago, when I first visited the docks, I was nervous. I wasn't thinking of Hart Crane, and I wasn't afraid of being beaten or robbed. When a sailor glanced at me, I walked away. I was married then, too, and wished more than anything that I'd nodded and stayed.

"We're here," the driver said.

I paid him and asked if he knew of a hotel nearby. He was from India or Pakistan and wore a dark purple turban. There were beads around the edges of the partition that separated him from the back seat. The cab smelled of clove.

"Hotels. You go that way." He pointed east.

I stopped two men in black leather jackets and pants. One wore a leather cap with a shiny visor, and the other was completely bald, his head polished.

"You guys know the Lure?'

The bald one turned and pointed. "Down the street," he said. "An old warehouse on your right, you'll see it."

They were on their way before I could say thanks.

The Lure was closed, its windows painted black. Graffiti was written across part of the brick front: EMINEM, SUCK THIS. There was a discrete sign in small block letters on the door: OPEN AT 9 P.M. MASK NIGHT.

I walked along 13th, then turned north on Eighth Avenue to look for a room and entered the heart of Chelsea. The sidewalk was lined with retro diners and Thai rooms, video stores, clothing boutiques, java bars, Korean delis, haunts for bric-a-brac. Some couples I passed walked hand in hand as if they believed they'd spend their lives together, two men in love as if they were entitled to their happiness when they were born. I thought about the men I might have loved.

In one of the storefronts two mannequins in black leather thongs were bound to each other with chains across their chests. It was called Cellar Stories. To the right of the entrance sat a young man with bright-red hair—curly and cut short—freckles all over his face. He was perched on a stool behind a glass case. He wore a navy muscle shirt that revealed tight, red, curly chest hair. His nipples were hard as drawer pulls. The right one had a ring on it that made a little O impression in the shirt. He was reading some play.

He looked up, nodded, and returned his attention to his book.

"I'm browsing," I said.

"Store's all yours," he said without raising his head.

In the case were about a dozen handcuffs, most of them silver, but one with a black leather pad wrapped around part of the cuff. I remembered the handcuffs in the bowl below the inflated Betty Boop in Stephen's apartment. *Were they just another piece of bric-a-brac? Or did he like to use them? Did he like to be shackled sometimes when he got fucked?* I knew so little about him, and somehow he'd become so central to everything. *If you play with the hand-cuffs would that be enough? Would you get tired of playing and want something more, something criminal? Was the fire-fighter into things he couldn't control?*

Scattered around the cuffs were poppers in small brown glass bottles, the kind found in old apothecary shops, and in the back of the case a sign in red block letters: SALE: ENFORCERS AND ENHANCERS HALF OFF.

The store was long and narrow. The first floor was filled with black leather jackets, vests, and pants. Boxes of combat boots were piled against one of the walls and a military-style gas mask hung nearby. There was a table covered with a mound of black leather gloves, some with fingers; others with just palms, like a biker's gloves.

In the back was a shelf of Billy dolls, blond with sky blue eyes, ripped abs, and stunning arm muscles. His skin was smooth, his lips curled into a killer smile. A card warned customers not to undress Billy in the store. But yes, it said, he's anatomically correct. He's out and proud. San Francisco Billy, Cowboy Billy, Master Billy, Sailor Billy, Leather Billy, Wall Street Billy. An entire militia of Billies.

Near the dolls were racks of cards: James Dean every-where, naked butts and cocks, pairs of men in tuxedos at the altar, men climbing naked out of pools and lakes and oceans. Nearby was a shelf of gay takeoffs on Twister, Clue, and Monopoly.

I wanted to find the masks and was going to ask the clerk when I noticed a narrow, black, iron spiral staircase leading downstairs. I could see, from the opening in the floor, a table covered with masks of all kinds.

Some were more severe than I'd thought possible. I

found one with laces like stitches that left parts of the ears exposed. There was a hood with zipper eyes and a full-face one with a spiked collar and chains. And a double-face hood—a thonged leather mask with eye- and mouth-holes and laced at the back, covered by an outer hood with no eye-holes and an all round zip. Even an executioner's. I picked out a simple black leather one that reminded me of a bat with its wings spread.

I held it against my face and breathed in the smell of leather. It was exciting. I looked through a rack of harnesses, all black leather, some with chrome chain and clip fasteners, others with rivets and buckles, an Adonis pouch and adjustable bum straps. Open- and closed-back ones, with hundreds of tiny pins on the inside of the straps. Some with a detachable codpiece.

The sign above one rack said HEAVY ENCLOSURE. This was even more extreme gear: a rubber bib-and-brace suit with waders, a suit with a zipper from collar to crotch and an optional gas mask (Israeli-made). There was even a rubber sleep sack, with a photograph of a man curled into it, zipped arm slots for restraints, no airholes visible. I thought of Stephen Hart, bagged and wheeled out of his apartment on a gurney. On my way out I passed a table covered with butt plugs and other anal toys: a half-dozen cue balls roped together in a row, fleshy rubber shapes that looked like small lava lamps, and fat jell sticks. Behind the staircase was a library of videos I hadn't noticed when I walked down: *Naked Sword, Hunting of the Russian Boy, All Twinks, Bare Celebs.* One row was labeled THE DICKS 'N' BOYS COLLECTION.

"Just a mask today," the clerk said. *Endgame,* the play he'd been reading, was closed beside the cash register.

"Nell and Nag," I said.

"Great, aren't they? I wish I could stuff my fuckin' parents in a trash can."

"It's a funny play."

"Yep. I'm working backstage on it over at St. Mark's."

"Good luck."

"That's $23.65."

I gave him cash.

"Do you have any chains with knives attached to them?"

"Knives?"

"Like a Swiss Army, the combination set, with corkscrew, can opener, file—a Boy Scout kind of thing."

"This isn't the Army-Navy. No knives. What about a whip, real horsehair?"

What could I do to the killer with a whip? "Not Boy Scout enough," I said.

He looked at me and said, "You like the boys."

He bagged the mask and handed it to me. He smiled. I left without answering

I didn't have any idea of how I'd find a weapon. *An ice pick,* I thought, *might be easy to get. Jesus, what am I becoming?*

I passed a place called the Big Cup with a gigantic white coffee cup hanging over the sidewalk from the storefront. Inside were men—most young and a few others my age— sitting on couches or at small tables. Some were alone reading newspapers and magazines, others talked to lovers or friends. There wasn't one woman in the café. *All these men are probably happy. At the very least they're living honestly, for anyone to see. I could have been one of them if I hadn't been so afraid. Maybe when it's all over…* I didn't know how to finish the thought.

I pictured Jared seeing his father put a hand down a man's pants. *Maybe—father, like son. You just don't go down on a friend in a cruiser and say it won't happen again. Maybe he's been hiding, too. Maybe there's a chance we can work things through. I'll call him. I'll say I didn't have a choice about meeting the killer. I might be able to do what he wants by myself. He would understand. He'd have a newfound respect. Who knows what might happen then?*

I decided I wouldn't call until I'd met the bastard. I felt like I couldn't risk Jared's intervention.

I looked around the Big Cup. No one noticed me. If he were there, he didn't give me a sign. It was 7:15. The club opened at 9; I decided to find a room.

A couple blocks away was a hotel above a gay bar named the Anaconda. The neon sign that climbed up most of the building's second floor just said HOTEL. Part of the O was missing so that it looked like a new moon, a lonely parenthesis. A separate door next to the bar entrance led up a steep flight of stairs that reminded me of the bathhouse in Providence. The lobby was about the size of a double room. The clerk, a man my age in a black T-shirt, sat behind the counter. He had tremendous biceps and a goatee with small patches of gray in it. Behind him was a row of clocks set to the times of hideaways across the world: London's Hampstead Heath, Mykonos, Amsterdam's Vondel Park, Rome's Monte Caprino, Bangkok, the Castro, Chelsea.

"I'd like a room," I said.

"Alone?"

"Yes."

"Do you want our president's suite?" He laughed.

"Just a single room."

"They're all alike, honey."

He didn't seem the type of guy who'd call someone honey. I was surprised because I liked it.

The walls were lined with black and white photographs of men in uniforms: bikers, athletes, police, men from all of the military branches, construction workers, a circle of bishops. There were three red vinyl chairs torn in places and patched with black electrical tape. On a couple of shabby end tables were metal scallop-shell ashtrays full of ashes, butts, chewed gum.

"That's $97.77," he said. "We like our guests to pay at check in. Credit card is OK."

I fished out my card. While he processed it, I was thinking how in the world I ever ended up here on a night like this.

"Hey, guy," the clerk said. "Here's your card." I signed the receipt. *Why didn't I give him cash?*

"Checkout is noon. Anytime after that the boss charges you for a whole day." He looked like he might want to flirt. I think I thanked him before I walked away, but I wasn't certain.

■

My room was on the fourth floor of the five-floor walkup. It was the kind most people rent late at night and stay in for a few hours. I suspected the odor of tobacco and sex never left it. A beat-up television with a rabbit ears antenna sat on a dresser too small for it in front of a mirror that was filled with the reflection of the bed. A water glass covered with a whitish film that looked like toothpaste rinse lay on its side next to the TV. In the bathroom were a sink, a toilet with a cracked seat, and a shower, all pre–World War II, with 1-by-1-inch black-and-white tiles covering the walls and floor. The faint odor of disinfectant couldn't mask the staleness all around. There was no globe on the light above the sink, and below the bulb was a mirror about the size of a plate, with black specks in places where the silver backing had worn off. It was the kind of place Travis Bickel would have called home.

I lay on the bed and looked at the cracks in the ceiling. The room was hot and dry—nosebleed air. *If I were going to kill him, I should have, at the very least, brought a knife. I should have found a gun somewhere. I should have prepared.*

I wasn't going to kill him. When I returned, I'd tell Jared that we had to reveal everything we knew. I imagined I would reason with the maniac when I met him at the Lure. I would say I understood, I sympathized. I wouldn't talk about evil or the absence of conscience. I wouldn't mention the beatings he gave his lover. I would tell him I shouldn't have gone home with Stephen Hart. I would try to make him believe I cared about his situation. I was someone he could trust. Maybe the thrill of murdering didn't sustain him, maybe the good man in him was tormented, and he could reclaim his conscience if he surrendered himself to the police. Even Jeffrey Dahmer apologized. Maybe killing for him wasn't like walking outside on a clear day.

I reached Bellemy on the cell.

"Sam Winchel's nowhere to be found," he said.

"I know. A detective here told me no one at his paper's heard from him in days."

"That's good information from a continent away."

I didn't say anything.

"The other two reporters, they check out. The *Sun*'s Jarzembeck died in a car crash just last night. Fuckin' drunk driver. And Sanchez at the *Daily Times* is in Mexico City covering some kind of immigration thing. He's been there for two weeks. The editors wanted to keep it quiet, but I found out from a couple of columnists. Favors all around."

"Did you find a photo of Winchel?"

"Not yet. He's pretty reclusive for a reporter. Enger isn't too interested in Winchel. He's back to thinking you're the top of the list."

I didn't answer.

"Where are you?" he asked.

"Home."

"Why is the call so scratchy?"

"What?"

"You said you were going to level with me. Now you're making me think I shouldn't be trying to help."

"I'm home, on the cell."

"You're lying again." Then he paused, and said, "Someone from Providence is looking for you. He wouldn't give me his name. He wanted to know if I'd talked to you today. What's going on?"

I told him I was losing the connection—I'd call him back later—and said goodbye. I was too unnerved to say anything more. *Jared's the only one who knew about Bellemy. He's trying to find me. Maybe meeting this bastard tonight is a mistake.*

I tried to picture the killer again: He would be handsome because Stephen Hart wouldn't take home just anyone. He wouldn't have a beard, not even a smartly trimmed one, because a beard hides too much and doesn't inspire trust. He'd have a hint of innocence in his eyes—someone a little nervous. He'd be a seamless liar. He'd be confident as stone and disguise arrogance with a silky tenderness. In a world of self-involved deceivers, he would appear the openhearted one. He was the perfect predator.

I called Sarah in Tampa. She answered the phone, expecting, I could tell, to hear from me. Before I hung up, I heard her say, "Dan, is that you?" *They're there; they're OK.*

The light in the room shifted from dusk to the glare from

the streetlights and the neon of the ASSOCIATED SUPER-MARKET across from the hotel. I was still lying on my back. The bedspread smelled stale, too. I turned my head and buried my face in it. I wondered whether it was the smell of accumulated semen—months of ejaculations, maybe years. I didn't know what the fuck to do. I felt sick.

■

It was 9 when I woke. My head faced the window and the lights of the city at night streamed in. I was surprised that I was hungry. I turned on the television and the snowy picture showed the pope holding up the Host during a rerun of Easter Mass in St. Peter's Square. He was speaking Italian in his Polish accent, his voice frail and tinny, but it was easy to gather what he was saying: "This is the body of Christ. Take this and eat it. Do this in remembrance of me." I took off my clothes and looked at my naked body in the mirror. The thought of death came so clearly that it didn't worry me. Its revelation had nothing to do with the pope or the killer who would be waiting for me at the Lure. I saw it like a driver sees a road lamp go suddenly dark along an empty highway on a pitch-black night.

After I showered, I remembered I hadn't brought a change of clothes. I decided not to wear my T-shirt. I put on my old boxers and socks, my denim shirt, L.L. Bean khakis—all ridiculous for the Lure, but on mask night the men might not notice. At a small shop a block from the hotel I ate a piece of pizza covered with oily green and red peppers and drank a Coke. I could have grabbed the knife beside a pie on the counter and slipped it beneath my jacket without anyone seeing, but instead I walked past it. *I can't kill him, not with a pizza knife, not with anything.* Outside, I hesitated and a man brushed against me. "Fuck you," he said. I realized it wasn't meant for me; he said it again and again as he walked on.

It was a little after 10 when I returned to the Lure. A dozen men—all in black leather jackets, some in leather pants, a couple in chaps with their butts exposed—were waiting in line. The doorman was checking IDs and making certain everyone had a mask or hood. Inside the door a counter with a sign on it said CHARITY NIGHT: COVER $3 TO BENEFIT NYC AIDS HOSPICE.

The man ahead of me had a mark on his neck he'd tried to cover with makeup and I wondered whether he was sick. I smiled at him stupidly and was glad he didn't see it. I wondered whether the virus was proliferating in my blood, streaming through my pancreas and liver, the arteries into my heart, the vessels to my brain. I pictured the gaunt Rock Hudson, Tom Hanks in a hospital johnnie in *Philadelphia,* the skeletal bodies of young African men.

"Hey, guy," I heard someone say. He was the man at the counter in a white T-shirt and black leather vest.

Maybe three feet separated us. I didn't look back to see whether the men behind me were irked.

"Sorry," I said.

"Three bucks," he said. "You know, we have a store right there on the right. You can buy some pants and chest gear if you want. It might help you get to know people better."

"Thanks." I gave him the money.

Before letting me pass, he said, "Put it on."

He was looking at the mask in my hand. I slipped it on and snapped it closed in the back.

"Better already," he said.

The mask felt sexy. I was surprised the leather wasn't really restricting. I wondered what the men in hoods felt, the men with the side laces drawing their ears back against their heads, the men with collars and spikes and rings around their necks, the men with chains dangling from their collars being pulled along by masters. I wished I didn't think my mask felt sexy. *I'd be a slave.*

The Lure was vast. I stood against a pillar near the entrance, not far from the first bar. The place was more crowded than I'd expected for Easter Sunday. The bartenders were shirtless and wearing briefs, one in just a jockstrap. Porn played on televisions bolted to the walls like monitors announcing flight departures and arrivals. An S/M film: men in masks and chains gathered in a cellar. One man fucked another while a third lay between their legs, raising his torso like a gymnast to suck the guy who was getting fucked. The actors didn't look different from most of the men around the bar, and for a moment I thought the televisions were closed-circuit. When I looked around, I saw I was the only one watching the movie.

I ordered a Bushmills from the bartender in the jockstrap. When he turned and reached for the bottle, I noticed a birthmark that looked like the shape of Nantucket on his ass. At first I thought it might have been a tattoo. He was wearing a hood with an open V in the center that started at his chin and ended right along his brows. He put down my whiskey and watched me drink it all in one swill. I asked for another and he poured it in the same glass. *I'd better be careful the old compulsion doesn't return. Not here, not tonight, not with the sick fuck watching.*

When I paid, he looked at my shirt and said, "You need some leather below the neck." He didn't smile, and turned to get someone a beer. I left the whiskey on the bar.

I walked to the shop and bought leather pants and a leather vest to wear over my shirt.

"There's a dressing room to the right," the clerk said as he swiped my credit card through a machine. He was a dwarf and sat on a barstool behind the cash register. His mask was Venetian, with a long bird's beak. His fingers were short and fat. He had spiked black hair. He wore a tight black T-shirt emblazoned with a gigantic red spider, its legs reaching out from a white web in the center. When I leaned over the counter to sign the receipt, I saw a leather pouch with a zipper covering his cock.

"You like it," he said.

"Sorry. I didn't mean to stare."

"You can't have what's in it, but if you want one, they come in one-size-fits-all, right over there."

I smiled.

In the dressing room, I decided not to wear my shirt under the vest. For the first few seconds the leather felt like a sheet of ice melting on my skin. I buckled it from bottom to the top. My chest hairs stuck out where the leather ended below my neck. I took off my khakis and stepped out of my boxers. I looked like a stranger, almost sinister, sexy. I pulled the pants up to my waist, buttoned the fly, and snapped it shut. The leather tightened and exaggerated my cock.

If I let myself drink more whiskey, I'll be lost. That's what he's counting on.

I asked the clerk for a bag for my clothes.

"Now your ass looks right tight, Daddy," he said, handing me a black plastic one. "The check is that way."

The coat check ran the length of a wall. There were two pool tables at each end and raised blocks for seats that formed an open rectangle around the room. Smoke swirled under florescent tubes in black metal hoods over the tables. I recalled the sight of the firefighter with a cue stick in his hand. *I could have taught him the song game. He could have played it someday with Jamie.*

I looked around. The killer could have been anyone watching from a perch on the blocks. He could have been keeping time to the music with combat boots. He could have been bare-armed and bare-assed, with a collar around his neck and chains dangling down his sides. He could have been goddamned anyone. All I knew was that he was watching.

The men against the wall were cruising everyone in the coat-check line. Their attention felt like a hand on the back of my neck. Hooded and masked men stared from eye-holes. No one seemed nervous. They were thinking of the sting of whips and the bite of ropes, of sticking their cocks into strangers' asses. Some were probably thinking about me. I didn't let my gaze rest on anyone for long, because I didn't want the murderer to infer my vaguest interest in anyone. But I wanted to see him. I wanted to let him know how much I despised him. I wanted to tell him I would kill him if I could.

When I reached the coat-check counter, I saw an envelope with my name on it.

"Who gave you this?" I asked the guy who took my coat and bag of clothes.

"What?" he said.

"This envelope."

"I didn't see it there until you mentioned it. Maybe it fell out of your coat."

He handed me a metal slug with a hole in it and the number 476 stamped into it, and then he took my stuff to a rack. I found an empty spot near an emergency exit and opened the envelope.

The note said: "Leather pants over your bare bottom? I'm surprised. Mix it up a little and maybe we'll talk."

He was reading me perfectly.

Someone in a leather mask like mine came up beside me.

"Hey, bat eyes," he said.

He was big, bearish—a wrestler's build. He had thick brown hair, some gray streaks. He wore a black muscle shirt and leather pants with a wide belt lined with silver studs. He had black cowboy boots. I was nervous. *He could be the killer. How was I going to know?*

"I guess there's a narrow range of originality in masks and hoods," I said, stupidly.

What am I doing? If I'm not careful, if this guy's not the killer, he could be next.

"I haven't seen you before," he said.

I didn't say anything, hoping he'd leave.

"Funny how you get to know the guys who come here Sundays, even though they're hooded or masked. Almost like mask night is set up to cater to a kind of open anonymity. I'm a professor at Fordham. How about you?"

"I'm waiting for someone," I said.

He touched the top snap of my vest. "Look at those sexy chest hairs standing at attention."

"Fuck off," I said, low enough so no one else could hear. I walked away. If the killer noticed, he'd think the guy was a loser. He wouldn't be interested.

It was almost 11 and the Lure was filling up fast. With more men—all in uniform—streaming in, it would be harder to keep track of anyone. I caught sight of someone on all fours near the bar. His master stood beside him holding the chain that tethered them. The slave looked up, waiting for something. When his master leaned over to hand him a beer, the guy dropped on his bare ass to the floor and took a drink. *The sick fuck is watching. He wants me to understand I'm his slave.*

I moved to another room where men were packed together like concertgoers. I couldn't see the attraction. I looked back to see whether I could notice someone advancing with me, but everyone looked the same. I moved farther into the room and saw the spectacle: Three men stood about six feet apart from each other, naked except for a thong or jock strap. Their hands were bound to brass rings that hung from a bar suspended from the ceiling. Hooded men in combat boots whipped them hard enough to cause welts to bubble on their backs.

I didn't leave. The three slaves wanted the gathering spectators to be part of their pleasure; we were a reason they endured pain. Two were silent when they were lashed; the third moaned. I felt suddenly nervous because the spectacle excited me. I remembered de Sade and wondered, *What's happening?* Onlookers were quiet except for a scattered few who talked as if they didn't notice what was going on. I wondered whether the sick fuck knew I'd react this way. *This is what he expects. And here I am, giving him what he wants. Jesus, in a former meat-packing warehouse.*

The music and the masks, the leather and the flesh, the sound of the men being flogged were hypnotic. I wanted to leave, but he'd told me to stay at least until midnight. He wanted me to choose someone special. He said he didn't like fems. He said he'd hurt my family if I didn't obey.

I decided I needed the drink. I ordered a Bushmills, and a man with a featureless mannequin mask walked up and offered to buy me another one.

"Just got this," I said.

"I've been watching you a while," he said.

He can't be the bastard.

"That's a little creepy, isn't it? Watching someone you don't know."

He was reserved, shy enough to make me certain he wasn't the killer. But interested enough to flirt.

"Everyone's watching everyone here. Maybe I should have said I think you're handsome."

"You look familiar." I wanted to make certain he wasn't the killer. *I have to be careful; he's the type the maniac would like.*

"You're joking, right. I'm wearing a mask with a blank expression." He laughed, muffled under the mask.

I knew I'd have to leave before the sick fuck saw us together.

"You're not a New Yorker, right?" he asked.

I didn't say anything.

"I can tell," he said.

"Look, I have to take a piss."

"Wait a second." He touched my arm. "Don't worry about this weird mask. I'm a cop. What's your name?"

From the neck down, he was covered in Army camouflage. *A cop? This isn't happening.*

"Daniel," I said.

There was something about him that kept me there, despite the danger I was putting him in. Foolishly, I believed he could help somehow.

"Are you into this stuff big time?" he asked.

"What stuff?"

"The masks, leather, the *chains*."

"It's the first time I've been in a pair of leather pants."

"Really. Well, you look good. I'm not a fanatic about the gear, and if I had a choice, I think I'd rather meet a guy in a bar where I didn't have to be in a butch uniform."

He had blue eyes. I wanted to believe that if he was a cop, he could protect himself.

"So you're afraid of being seen by someone you know," I said.

What if he is *the guy?*

"I guess so. I'm not out on the force. I don't want to deal with the hassle. That's all. Hey, what about you?"

I looked around to see whether I could notice someone watching. *He's telling the truth. If I don't move now, he'll be killed.* I was visibly nervous.

"Look, that piss. I'll be back."

"Wait." He lifted his mask to reveal his face. The space between us was so close that the bottom of his mask touched my eyebrows.

"See. I'm not hiding some hideous disfigurement."

I felt his breath on my face.

He moved the mask to the side, and before I could pull back, he kissed me.

"I just wanted to do that. Take the chance that you might decide to really come back and talk to me some more when you get finished in the can. Tell you the truth, I've kind of surprised myself too."

I turned away and left him and didn't look back. He called after me to say his name was Sean. *If the psycho saw the kiss, the cop would have to take care of himself. He's not stupid. He wouldn't put himself in jeopardy like some dumb-ass lonely fuck who lets his dick get him into trouble. What if he isn't a cop? What if he's the guy?*

There was a crowd in the john. On the walls above the five urinals closest to the back were video cameras aimed at the men's cocks, taping as they pissed so that people at the bars could see the live water shows. A sign on the wall said: IF YOU'RE CAMERA SHY, DON'T PISS INTO ONE THROUGH FIVE. A long red arrow below the words pointed left. The lines behind those were very long.

I looked back to see whether the cop had followed me in. He wasn't there. I felt a finger on my ass and decided to ignore it. But he must have mistaken my obliviousness for an invitation because his fingers brushed past my hip and rested on my buttoned fly. His breath scraped my neck. Inches behind me, he leaned closer and slid his tongue along my skin. The other men in the bathroom must have thought he was my lover, or my night's good luck. He unfastened a button. I felt his fingers press my cock as he threaded something rubbery through the buttonhole. He cupped his hand over my balls and then he walked away. By the time I turned around, all I could see was the back of his black leather hood and the top of his black jacket. He looked like everyone else in a phalanx of men who'd just walked in. I tried to run after him but I couldn't break through the crowd. I noticed a condom hanging from the buttonhole. My hand trembled while I pulled it out. It was crumpled, sticking together with what must have been old semen.

I shouted, "Let me by!"

Eye-holes everywhere turned and watched me paw through the black leather mass. I stumbled over a chain hanging from a slave on his hands and knees and hit my head hard against the corner of a metal sink.

I was dizzy. The floor felt like it was quaking. The nerves behind my eyes stung and a light like a flashbulb snapped somewhere inside my skull. Someone helped me to my feet and led me to the corner by the door.

"You've got a cut," a man said through the mouth hole of an executioner's mask.

I put my hand, the one with the condom in it, against my forehead.

"Get him some paper towels," he said.

A man in a leather harness with his ass pulled up like a marionette handed me a fistful of brown paper.

"I'll be OK," I said.

"Someone call an EMT," the executioner said.

"No, I'm OK. It's superficial."

I've got to find him. I held the bunched-up paper towels against my forehead.

"I'm OK," I repeated.

"I'll help you out," he said, putting his arm around my back. I smelled sweat and tobacco on his body. A stud on his nipple pressed into my armpit and hurt.

"No," I said, and broke free.

I walked out to a corner of the poolroom and sat against the wall. I held the paper against my cut, hoping it wasn't serious. The man in the executioner's hood followed me out and saw me sitting down. He shrugged and walked away.

He's about six feet tall. I looked around for other black hooded men. From my seat, I counted 20 men in hoods about that height. The music hurt my head. I remembered his breath against my neck. I removed the clump of papers from my forehead. The bleeding had stopped. I picked the condom from the bloody towels. There were splotches of dried blood on the latex. I stuffed it into my vest pocket and leaned back against the wall. The room was reeling. I looked up. The ceiling was black metal, embossed vines and leaves swirled inside metal squares. Below writhed the same mass of black leathered men hoping for something (at least forgetfulness) inside the Lure's vast night.

I stood, wobbly for a moment, and searched for the cop who'd kissed me. *I've got to warn him. What the fuck have I done?*

Every room was so packed I moved in intervals of inches. The cop wasn't at the bar where I'd left him. He wasn't anywhere. I panicked. *They'd left together.*

I asked the doorman whether he saw someone in a hood leave with a guy wearing a mannequin mask.

He gave me a look and turned away.

I searched the rooms again, hoping the killer might reveal himself. *Maybe the cop left alone. Maybe I didn't put him in jeopardy, too.* I picked up my clothes from the coat check and struggled through the Lure one more time, but still I didn't see him. I walked to Ninth Avenue and waited for a cab and scanned the street. No one I recognized anywhere. *Why didn't I warn him?* My head hurt so much I squeezed my eyes shut. *He's a cop, he'll be OK.* A cab stopped, and I told the driver to take me Penn Station.

"You've been to the Lure?" he asked.

I didn't say anything, and he didn't let my silence deter him.

"I've been there," he said. "Never on mask night."

I realized I was still wearing the mask, unsnapped it, and put it on the seat. I didn't want a conversation.

"I hear some important people go there Sunday nights. Doctors, priests, Wall Street execs. It's the anonymity. A guy can hide and get some ass. You want to go somewhere private? I could give you a blow job."

When I didn't answer, he stopped talking. He pulled up to Pennsylvania Station, and I handed him a ten. At nearly 2 in the morning, the place was empty except for street people, janitors, policemen, a few passengers waiting for early-morning trains. A cop tapped the feet of a homeless man asleep in a chair in the departure area. I went into a bathroom stall, changed into my denim shirt and khakis, leaving the leather vest and pants on the floor. On my way out I remembered the condom and returned to fish it out of the vest. I slipped it into a back pocket and thought about washing up. A cop at a sink splashed water on his hair and slicked it back with a comb. If he noticed my bloody forehead, he wasn't interested. I left with the smell of blood still

171

on me. *Maybe Jared is right. Maybe killing this bastard is what we have to do.* I heard the announcement for the Boston-bound train and headed for the gate.

On the way to Providence I tried to make sense of everything. *Is that all he wanted? Maybe it's all over.* I remembered the killer's breath on my neck. *No, he's not finished.*

Somewhere in Connecticut I nodded off. In my sleep I still felt him fingering my cock.

monday morning

After the train pulled in I walked up College Hill to Prospect Terrace. It was a little after 6. I sat on the same bench close to the stairs that led to the base of Roger Williams's pedestal. I thought about the kid who'd held a knife to my thigh and the photograph that the sick fuck took and left for Sarah and Jamie. From the bench I watched the founder's arms outstretched, passing stony judgment on Providence.

I called Jared's cell, but he didn't answer. I tried his house and left a message: "Reach me at home in about an hour. I want to do everything I can."

He'd be surprised.

First, he'd have to arrange protection for Sarah and Jamie in Tampa. He'd find out whether the cop from the Lure turned up dead with a condom pinned to his chest. *Jesus, no,* I thought. *Not another one.*

A few people walked into a church along North Main at

the bottom of the hill. They looked small and far away. *Soon he'll be sending me another souvenir.* I'd been to this park a hundred times, but never in the early daylight when the city seemed so undisguised, when I wasn't looking for someone looking for sex. *This is my punishment for a life that wasn't true. This is providence?* Bells tolled from the high church steeple. I so often began my thinking with His name: Jesus this and Jesus that. I didn't think He mattered much to me anymore, not even naked on the cross, not even on the day after He'd risen out of the tomb. My daughter told me she preferred Zen. I was so tired I could have stretched out on the bench and slept. Instead I walked home.

The patrolman must have recognized me walking up the road because he got out and waited.

"Lots of people have been looking for you," Lambert said. He was the cop who'd taken Aidan home and later fetched the hankie-code man's hand from Chelsea. He was someone Jared trusted.

"Where's Jared?"

"He's home."

"I called. He didn't answer."

"He was out most of the night looking for you. I'll raise him."

"Did you hear anything about my wife and daughter?"

"They've gone to Tampa. At least that's what Serio said."

"Who?"

"The patrolman outside the house last night. He took them to the airport."

I was relieved the good cop had taken them and wished he'd been there when I got back. He wasn't all business like Lambert. I would have been able to confide in him. He would have given me details about Sarah and Jamie. He would have remembered whether they walked arm in arm to the cruiser, or whether one of them had lingered behind, returning to the house for another look.

"What happened to your head?"

"I fell against a sink."

"There's dried blood all over the side of your face."

"I need to talk to Jared."

"I'll make some calls and find him."

I thought about Jared searching in the usual cruising places: Purgatory Chasm, the railroad tracks, Waterplace Park. *Why would he ever be interested in a coward like me?*

I was surprised the cop didn't ask where I'd gone. He was tall, blond, unexpectedly boyish-looking, considering his temperament. I could tell he understood more than he was letting on. I wondered whether he was gay too. *Maybe he's Jared's secret lover, maybe they're on a gay crusade.*

"Was there another murder?" I asked.

"Not so far."

"Good."

"What's good?"

"No murder."

"Right."

He leaned over the roof of his cruiser and watched me walk to the house. When I got to the door and looked back, he was on a cell phone, still watching me.

I yelled out: "Is that Jared?"

He shook his head no and waved at me to go inside.

■

The Sunday *Times* was undisturbed on the hutch next to the front door. *She didn't even take the magazine.* On the kitchen stove the bacon from the morning before was frozen in a pool of congealed grease. I couldn't remember another time when she'd left a mess like this. I recalled Sarah and Jamie standing next to the photograph from Prospect Terrace: "from a chum of your dad." I pictured his fingers on my cock and felt his breath on my neck. *Who?* I wondered. Still nothing clicked.

I thought about Jamie when she'd seen her father with his pants around his ankles and a boy not much older than her on his knees. Would she ever understand?

I imagined the last words of their conversation before they left for the airport, as if their anger held the sounds in place until my return released them. The house was emptier than it had ever been before and the years of complicated love were suddenly drawn out of it. In the upstairs bedrooms, there were a few pieces of clothing scattered around, and an air of vacancy was everywhere.

I noticed the clock on the night table next to our bed and realized that for days I'd had no steady grasp on time. It was 8 in the morning. Monday. The day after Easter. Real time. It was three and a half days since Stephen Hart had entered me in his bed in a city a continent away. It was hours after the murderer had threaded a condom through my buttonhole.

I went to the bathroom and washed the dried blood from my face. The water was cold and ran down my cheeks onto the white porcelain where it spread, a watery-rust color, before draining away. *He's winning. He's making his malice bearable, almost ordinary.*

The comforter was slightly rumpled where Sarah had fallen asleep. I lay down and smelled the scent of perfume she'd left there—one that didn't suggest excess, a whiff of shore breezes in August. I pictured the first time we made love, a February. We were seniors in high school and had driven out to her parents' cottage in Evangola on Lake Erie.

We built a fire in an iron wood stove set back into a fireplace in a room overlooking the dunes. In the distance, through a long picture window, we could see moonlight on the lake.

We stood in the center of the room on a white carpet that looked like it belonged almost anywhere else. The light came from a row of small candles across the mantel and the open stove door. Above the fireplace were three paintings of empty wooden skiffs—maybe the same small rowboat in each one—floating on the lake that reflected three differently hued skies.

She pulled my turtleneck over my head and kissed the center of my chest as if she'd done this before. Days later she told me she'd practiced undressing me in her mind because she'd wanted everything perfect. She knelt and unlaced my boots, and I stepped out of them without her telling me to. I touched her hair, and we still hadn't said a word. I made love to her because I couldn't disappoint her—the first in an endless succession of deceptions. She rose and kissed me while she moved her hand down my back and across my belt. She felt my cock through my jeans and unbuttoned them and slid them down to my ankles. She pulled down my briefs and said, "There, now step out." I obeyed. I always obeyed.

Those were the only words we spoke until the first time ended. Or maybe she said she loved me. I was too afraid to say anything, and clumsy at sex, and worried that I hadn't satisfied her. The second time that night I lasted longer. And in the morning longer still. I didn't tell her about the dream that stirred me awake while her head was tucked against my side: a locker room at the school gymnasium, two boys I didn't know, everyone naked and afraid to look at one another. I woke from the dream with a hard-on, and when we made love I pictured one of the boys sucking me. For years when we made love, I pictured him. I was that low, even when we were young.

◾

The phone rang. It was Jared.

"You met him in New York. For Christ's sake, *a cop*."

"How do you know?"

"An NYPD detective called about a half hour ago. The stiff had some kind of mask on and was wearing camouflage. The rubber badge was pinned on his chest. A cop, for Christ's sake. They found him about 3 in the morning under a lamppost in Battery Park. New York already knows about the connection to our condom killer."

"Who gave him that name?"

"What name?"

"Condom killer: It makes him seem like he isn't real."

"What's wrong with you?" he asked, the irritation mounting in his voice.

"So the NYPD knows. Good. That means we can get their help. Enger's coming too."

"New York doesn't know shit about you, and maybe we can keep it that way."

"I think that's a good idea."

He wasn't listening. He said, "Our best shot is finding him before he goes underground."

"I said I think you're right. I'm willing to try whatever you think will make him stop."

He paused for a moment. Then, without really acknowledging my newfound conviction, he said, "I know what I'm doing. I control the chain of evidence here. We'll make this happen. Don't worry."

Unlike before, his voice seemed strangely detached. He said, "The detective was disarticulated."

I heard him but didn't let it register until later. I was rethinking my acquiescence. I pictured the killer's corpses one by one. I thought about the empty skiff in the painting in the cottage at Evangola. I pictured Jared the night we met, and I wanted to love him.

"The cop kissed me in the Lure. That's why he's dead," I said.

"Why the fuck did you let him do it?" he asked. "Sometimes I think you're looking for trouble."

He'll never love me.

"What's his name?" I asked.

"Who?"

"The dead cop."

"You let a guy kiss you in a bar and you don't find out his name. What's going on inside your head?"

He was more animated now, more like himself. I was going to say I remembered it was Sean.

"His name was Shepard, a cop for 20 years."

"Jesus."

He could tell I was getting more and more confused. He said, "Get some sleep. Even a couple hours will help. When you wake, call your wife and daughter. They must be worried. I've got some things to work out with detectives here. I'll be over in a few hours."

I caught him just before he clicked off.

"Jared."

"Not now," he said. "Get some rest."

"I'm glad you're helping me like this."

"Why wouldn't I?" he said and then clicked off.

I kept the phone at my ear. I waited for his voice to return and remembered he said the cop's body was "disarticulated."

I looked up the definition: "to separate at the joints." *What kind of a word is* disarticulate? *Something a butcher might say, a surgeon, a pathologist, a serial murderer.* I pictured the body strewn under the lamplight. Why did he use that word on the phone? It's not the kind of thing you say out loud and leave there.

I forgot to ask him about the kid from the park. *If he's been killed, Jared would have said something. We're going to make sure this all ends soon.* I felt dizzy. The veins in my neck throbbed.

I hadn't noticed the red message light flashing.

The first was from Roger, who said he was worried. I wasn't acting like someone nominated for a prize. Then my daughter: "Dad, where are you? Are you OK? Call us, please." Next was Bellemy: "Look, I still don't think you're a killer. I'll be there Monday, sometime just after noon. I'm on a red eye. Enger's flying out at the same time. You've got to let me help. I'm not being selfless here. I'm thinking, story of my career." Jamie again: "Why haven't you called? I'm afraid he's hurt you. Please call." Then Sarah: "We're at mother's. Jamie doesn't know how to take what's happened. She's scared stiff you haven't called. I'm worried, too, about more than just you. I'm taking an early-morning flight back. Jamie will stay here. You better be home to tell me what the hell is going on."

I thought, *She can't be coming back, not to this. I'll call and tell her to stay in Tampa, and if she'd already left, I'd tell Jared to dispatch an officer to meet her plane and send her back.*

The last message bleeped on, received about 3 in the morning. The caller ID showed it was from Sean Shepard and gave his number, a 212 area code. A raspy voice: "Nice taste in men, chum. Thanks. Oh, and check your e-mail. I've got some work for you. Bye." I punched in the number and a recording said the cell phone of the customer I was trying to reach was turned off or out of signal range.

I clicked my mail server and his message was waiting:

> Follow these orders exactly or I'll be teed off. Didn't you know I have the patience of a tarantula? I'll find you fucking family anywhere. I'll wait a long time if I need to. Be good and do what I tell you.
>
> About 11 head off to the woods overlooking the Seekonk River. You've been there before, I know. It's a bright Monday, and men will be out for an early lunch break. Find a good-looking cruiser, someone young, about 20 to 35. Remember, no fems. Take him to the abandoned boathouse along the river. Inside, make sure he goes down on you because I want the taste of you inside his mouth. Maybe one day you'll let me taste it fresh? Fuck him, too, if you want. I've got time. Now pay attention: Restrain him, keep him quiet. You figure out the details. Then when you're sure he can't escape, you leave. I'll handle it from there. I hope you're up to the task, because the consequences of failing are very ugly. Bring in the cops and I'm done with you, too. All yours, Buddy

I realized he wanted me to do everything except kill for him.

■

Jared drove up the driveway in his Jeep Cherokee and walked back to the curb to talk to Lambert in the unmarked. He returned to the Jeep, took a green trash bag from the back, and passed it through the window. The cop drove off.

I met him at the door.

"What was in the bag?" I asked.

"Some stuff I found by the railroad tracks: a pair of pants, boxer shorts, shoes, long wool coat—all black. They might belong to the your park trick. They didn't look like they'd been there long. No body, though. No blood, either. Maybe he's just playing us with this one. I asked the patrolman to take them to the lab. See if we can lift anything that links it to the other killings. But clothes without a body—that's not his M.O."

I tried to remember whether I noticed the kid's shoes.

"What about the photograph? Can't you tell if those were his clothes?"

"What photograph?"

"The one the sick fuck took at the park. Sarah was supposed to give it to the cop who took them to the airport."

"She must still have it."

"Why would she forget something like that?"

"Maybe she didn't forget. Maybe she wants it for evidence in divorce court."

I gave him a look and said, "She wouldn't to that."

"I'll find out."

"Those clothes might not belong to the kid."

"Like I said, it's not his M.O. We can't be sure until the kid turns up alive, or as the next stiff. It would have helped if you knew the bastard's name."

He tried to reach Serio. I remembered the smell of mocha java wafting from the car window Saturday night.

Jared couldn't get him. This dispatcher said he and his family had left for Disney World.

"He didn't say anything about going away."

"Who the fuck do you think you are? His father?"

"There was a note. It said: 'Picture, a thousand words.'"

"And the photograph?"

I told him the kid was sucking me at the base of the statue. I said my pants were bunched around my ankles and that Sarah and Jamie were speechless when they saw it.

"At least he has a sense of humor."

"What's funny?"

"You, with your pants down," he said without hesitating. "Pathetic, too. What the fuck's wrong with you? This is what a celebrated columnist makes of himself? You better hope the media doesn't see it. They love to eat their own."

"It wasn't funny. Nothing's funny here."

He said, "You must have looked ridiculous."

He sounded disappointed, as if he realized I was someone he didn't really know.

I remembered I hadn't told Jared about the message on the machine and the latest e-mail.

"He's contacted me again," I said.

"Why didn't you tell me?"

"I found it on the machine after we talked."

I led him to the study and showed him the printout of the first e-mail summoning me to the Lure. I wanted to reveal everything at once. I told him about buying the mask. I said I'd thought about finding a weapon to kill the bastard. "I know you're right," I told him. "Maybe it would be better if we caught him dead." I described the detective flirting with me and how I couldn't find him again to warn him. "He's a cop. He should have been able to take care of himself," I said, my voice too shrill. I was becoming more and more unnerved.

I told him the killer walked up behind me in the bathroom, put his hand on my fly, and fingered one of the buttonholes. He touched my cock and breathed down my neck. Before I guessed he was the murderer, he'd gotten

away. I didn't know he'd threaded a condom in the buttonhole until I looked and saw it there.

I was breathless as I reached into my pocket and handed
him the condom.

Jared's eyes flickered with concentration.

"The fucker is taking chances because he knows he has to
scare the shit out of you. Maybe he isn't the typical loner.
Maybe he's someone you know." He dropped the condom
on my desk. "For Christ's sake. This thing's used."

"Sorry. I'm not thinking."

"You can say that again. Did you recognize his voice on
the machine?"

"He faked it, made it sound like gravel mixing in his
mouth."

Jared must have noticed I was coming undone because
he put his arm around my shoulder. His touch felt like abso-
lution. *He's a confessor, he's forgiven me.*

He looked at me closely and asked, "What happened to
your forehead?"

"I fell and hit a sink in the Lure. It's not so bad."

"You sure?" He put his hand against the cut. "Looks like
it sealed itself."

Is it possible I know this guy?

I said, "Maybe I'm just a part of the game, a facilitator, an
instrument he uses before he kills. Maybe I don't know him."

"Maybe he doesn't want to murder you. Not unless he
believes he has to."

"Then what do you think he wants?"

"To remake you."

"That's crazy. He doesn't give a shit about me *personally*.
Maybe he craves men and hates himself for it."

"Just like you," Jared said evenly. "You might be right.
Maybe he's attracted to you, and he doesn't like the impulse.

That's why he kills men you fuck. It's his way of punishing both his desires and you."

Why did he say the bastard's just like me?

"I don't fuck men. I'm not like him."

"Maybe he thinks you fuck *with* men. You're the columnist. People trust you, but he knows you're a liar. If he wants to own you, the only way he can is to scare you first. He thinks that once you understand him, you'll sympathize with him, maybe even admire him. And if not, it doesn't matter. Even if you hate him, he'll still own you because he knows you fear him."

"Where are you *getting* this?"

"I'm profiling. If he's not the type to go random, he's going to latch on to someone. Obviously he's picked you. I'm trying to figure out why."

"You think he's identified with me because I've been living a secret life too. Jesus, if something like this is true, he's not going to let go."

"That's why we have to make sure we stop him—and do it before the other investigations force him to act against you. He's not the type of serial who wants to get caught. But he wants his big prize, and that's you. We'll use that desire to catch him."

"If I know him, why haven't I been able to turn up a single suspect?"

"The Seattle firefighter? Tell me about this guy," he said.

"I found AZT in his medicine cabinet. I think he might have been positive."

"That's great. What other surprises are you keeping?"

I retrieved the pills from the desk and told him someone had left them on the floor outside the stall in O'Hare.

"Christ, why didn't you tell me?"

"I forgot."

"You *forgot?* What the fuck else have you forgotten to tell me?"

He asked whether there were other pills. I told him: aspirin, decongestants. "Why?"

"If he had HIV, there'd be other drugs—protease inhibitors. Nobody with HIV just takes the AZT anymore," he said.

"I know. All I remember is this bottle." I didn't understand why he was so interested.

"You're a dumb shit for somebody who's supposed to be so smart. Did you let this guy fuck you?"

I didn't answer. I looked at my watch. It was almost 9:30.

"He sent me orders," I said.

"Now what are you talking about?"

"He wants me to find a new trick in the woods along the river—by noon."

I clicked on the e-mail and showed it to Jared. I said, "This could be the opportunity you're looking for."

Chelsea barked. She was back at the door stoop.

"Do something about that dog," he said.

He read the e-mail and said, "You're right. This is it."

I didn't say anything.

"That dog's got to stop," he said.

He went to the door and said something to Chelsea. I thought I heard her whine. *Did he hit her?*

"Maybe we can trap him in the boathouse," I said when he returned.

"You're thinking more clearly now." He paused. "Maybe this guy thinks he loves you."

I said, "That's ridiculous."

"Why? It's like a stalker who thinks he knows someone famous he's never met. You're a writer, he reads your columns, you make him mad or maybe you intrigue him.

Soon he decides you're the one he wants to own. To him, ownership might be love. That's why he wants you to take the trick to the boathouse. He doesn't want to kill *you* there. He's got something else in mind."

His insistent profiling was excruciating. I was going to ask about the dog when he touched my arm.

"I'm telling you this guy knows you. He knows you from your columns. He knows your work," he said.

Maybe his father's murder is really part of this.

I said, "You think this guy killed your father, don't you? That's one of the reasons this is so personal."

"I told you I'm not interested in avenging my father's death. That careless fuck appeared out of nowhere. The deal here is this bastard, and his focus on you."

I didn't say anything else. It was satisfying to think Jared was doing this for me.

He read the second e-mail again. "What the guy says about your family. He means it. My guess is he's eventually going to hurt them. We have to make sure he doesn't."

"I know."

I thought about all of the men already dead and said, 'I'm sorry."

"Fuck, sorry. There will be a time for sorry later, but not now"

He noticed my somberness and said, "This is going to work."

"If it doesn't?"

"It will."

Jared told me he wanted a few minutes to think about the details. I turned on the CD player and listened to Maura O'Connell sing about the Isle of Malachy again. I pictured Jamie on the couch and wanted everything to be over.

After a few songs, Jared explained the trap. He said

Lambert was going to be the lure. He said I could trust the kid. They'd been working together for a couple of years, and besides: the kid was closeted, too. "You see," he said, "it's personal for everyone."

I'd meet him in the woods, just as the sick fuck wanted. I'd make a move, do something convincing, and Lambert would show he's interested. Then I'd lead him down the hill and across the street to the riverbank and the abandoned boathouse. Jared would already be inside, hiding somewhere.

Lambert would enter first. Inside, there'd be a struggle, and I'd pretend to hit him so that he'd be knocked out long enough to restrain him. He asked whether I had any duct tape, and I told him there was some in the garage. I'd have the roll in my pocket, and I'd tape Lambert's feet and hands and mouth so that he couldn't escape or scream. I'd leave, just like the bastard ordered. I'd climb back up the hill and walk home. He said the next time I'd hear from him, it would be over.

"And what about the maniac?"

"I told you I'll be hiding in the boathouse. I'll be there when you leave. When the bastard shows, I'll surprise him and take him down. If something goes wrong, there'll be backups waiting to move in."

"If something goes wrong?"

"Don't think about it. Nothing's going to go wrong."

Jared called Lambert and explained everything.

When he was finished, I asked, "What if one of us fucks up in the woods or on the way to the boathouse. What if we tip him off."

"Lambert's not going to screw up. He wants the bastard as much as anyone. He's going to do everything right, and so are you."

I didn't say anything.

"You know the woods and riverbank?" he asked.

"Yes."

"Figures. Every fag in Providence can walk it blindfolded."

His sarcasm surprised me.

"You understand—he would kill you eventually. Serials always kill the objects of their obsession."

"What if he doesn't show?"

He shrugged. "I'm betting he will. He wants to up the ante. He'll show."

I read his e-mail again. "Jesus. He says, 'Tell the cops and everything's finished.' He's talking about Sarah and Jamie."

"If we don't do this, they're finished for sure. Count on it."

He waited to see whether I'd respond. When I stood there silently, he said, "I'm going to help you get out of this, and it starts by catching the bastard before he destroys you and everything you care about."

I nodded. *If Jared would kiss me, I'd be convinced there might be a future to care about.*

down by the river

Lambert was leaning against a huge copper beech not far from the path running through the woods. He had a Buffalo Bills cap on backward, a sweatshirt with PROVINCETOWN printed on it, and jeans with a tear across part of his ass. They were wedged down so that you could see his white briefs sticking out. When I walked by, he smiled. I thought, *Any other time my heart might be racing for a different reason.*

I worried the sick fuck would be able to see my legs quivering. *I'm going to tip him off.*

I left the path and walked up to the young cop. I looked down and touched his crotch.

"You're handsome."

"That's original," he said, loud enough so that only I could hear. He smiled, put his hand on my ass, and said, louder now, "What do you like?"

"Almost everything. But not outside."

"Where?"

"What about the boathouse down the hill? The burnt-out one the Brown crew team used."

"Never been."

"Let's go."

It was that easy. My confidence surged. *It's really this easy.*

I looked around to see whether I might recognize the killer. Maybe he was one of the others cruising in the woods. No one clicked.

Lambert walked about three feet behind. A car drove by—a woman with a black Labrador beside her in the front seat. She was talking on a cell and didn't notice us. The dog didn't turn its head.

The door of the boathouse was jammed, but a window was knocked out, and Lambert pointed to it and climbed over the sill. I followed and scraped my kneecap on the splintered frame. I tumbled onto the floor, bracing myself with my hands so that my face missed the wet mud. The place smelled of rot and ash.

I saw Jared behind a chaotic pile of charred life preservers. He was wearing a tight gray T-shirt with PAW SOX written across it in large red letters. The muscles in his arms and chest surprised me. Before I could stand and catch my balance, he held up a gun with a silencer and fired once. The bullet struck Lambert in the center of the forehead and he collapsed into a stack of scorched oars, his eyes wide-open, stunned.

I stood and Jared grabbed me across the chest and rammed a knee into my groin. He took the duct tape from my pocket, wrapped a piece over my mouth, tied a rope around my chest and arms and lashed my ankles together. Everything happened so fast—my mind reeled. He took cuffs out of his pocket and cuffed my hands behind my back.

"Remember these?" he asked. "They belonged to your firefighter fuck."

He stood me up and leaned me against a wall. He tore off my shirt and threw it on top of the pile of oars where Lambert had fallen.

The floor felt like swamp mud underfoot. Jared drew his hand up my bare chest, around my neck and over my mouth.

"Jesus, no," I tried to say.

With his other hand, he unbuckled my pants, unzipped my fly, and pulled them, along with my shorts, down to my ankles. Then he grabbed my ankles and my feet left the ground. I fell, striking my head on the wreckage of a burnt rowboat. The bash felt like it drew blood. He climbed onto my chest so that I couldn't move.

"Jared," I whispered.

"You didn't know, did you?"

I felt his ass on my stomach. His shins pinned my shoulders in the muck. He wedged my neck between his knees so that it was hard to breathe. His breaths came easily.

"Don't make me break your arms."

He held my chin so that I was looking directly at him. With his other hand, he dragged over a black leather satchel that was lying nearby. He took out more duct tape and wound it tightly around my mouth and head. The tape pressed my ears against my skull and made his voice sound cavernous.

He rolled me onto my stomach and slid his knees down against my hips. I felt his breath on my neck as he leaned forward to retrieve something else from the bag. His breathing became more intense. He sat up, his ass pressing down on mine. He hammered the center of my back once with his fist—hard enough to knock the wind out of me. I lifted my face from the mud and chewed at the tape, gulping for air that wasn't there. When I breathed, it felt like specks of glass shot up my nostrils.

He tore something open—a packet—and dropped it on my back. Everything sounded like it was happening inside my skull. He undid his pants and pulled them down far enough so that he could wrest himself out of them while he remained on top of me. I felt his balls on my ass and his hard cock against the small of my back. He sat up again and was almost still. *A condom,* I thought. *He's putting on a condom.*

"So this is what *we* like."

Then he lunged, his chest hard against my back, his collarbone digging into me, his breaths primitive, lashing my neck. He tore two fingers into my ass and out again, then thrust his cock inside me. The pain obliterated everything for a moment. I turned my head and saw Lambert's body curled into a question mark atop the pile of oars.

Jared's breathing grew sinister, virulent with cruel pleasure. While he was fucking me, he made the first cut—a line across my shoulders. I almost didn't notice the sting, but I felt my warm blood gathering on my skin.

After he came, he collapsed on top of me and licked the back of my neck. He licked the line of blood across my shoulders, pressing his tongue into the wound. He let out a guttural sigh as his cock softened inside my ass. I wanted to appeal to him, but my voice was lost beneath the tape. He was still inside me.

I felt the tip of the blade against my skin below my armpit. I squirmed and realized I'd forced my body into it when I moved.

"See, if only you'd be docile. I was going to score a clean thin line like this."

I felt his cock slip out of me.

The blade ran lightly along the side of my ribs. He slid it along my skin without cutting me. He turned me over and I closed my eyes.

"I'm good enough with this to find your two floating ribs. The only two cut off from the blood supply. They begin about right here."

He pressed the point of the knife into my skin.

"I could have cut a radiate ligament here at the tip of the rib and vertebra, just so you know, and the pain would have been unbearable."

He slid the blade, lightly again, and paused along the top of my thigh. "You need this tensor fasciae latae to flex your thigh; it's important when you're fucking."

The blade ran along my crotch and he lifted it just as his fingers brushed my balls. I couldn't see it, but the blade felt thin and very sharp.

"Maybe just deep enough to draw a little more blood."

I felt the blade sting.

He leaned back and sat down on my cock. I tried to raise my head to see him. I wanted to plead with him, anything to make him stop.

He stood and kicked me below the rib cage. He knew where to knock the wind out of me. When I looked, he was pulling up his pants. He said, "Good fuck."

The instrument in his hand looked like a silver pen or air-pressure gauge, except its tip was a narrow blade. *It's the knife he used to cut off Stephen Hart's penis.* I wanted to close my eyes, but I thought, *That's what he's counting on, my massive capacity for inaction.*

I turned and curled my legs against my stomach and tucked my chin into my chest. He bent down and yanked my legs out and rolled me onto my back.

"Soft," he said. "I'm surprised; I thought you'd like it

rough. Most passive shits do. It's the theory of opposites."

I fought back a moan because I didn't want him to think I felt anything except disbelief. It was enough for him to see the utter astonishment in my eyes. I thought, *If I could just make him remember the night in the cruiser outside the warehouse 20 years ago, he'd let me live.*

He drove the toe of his boot into the center of my groin and the pain spiked up my spine and into my throat.

"Don't look at me like some hurt puppy dog. Don't think I give a shit."

I kicked my bound legs and thrust my shoulders and head into the muck, hoping, somehow, my convulsive actions would make him stop.

"You surprise me. I didn't think you'd put up a fight."

He sat on my chest and leaned forward. He reached into his back pocket and took out a plastic sandwich bag. He slapped the bag across my face a few times.

"Souvenir for your wife?"

He looked over at Lambert for the first time and said, "Piece of shit. Another sick closeted fag."

I closed my eyes. I decided I wasn't going to die in this burned-out boathouse, naked, writhing in the muck.

He reached for the knife again and pressed it into the duct tape. I felt the tip of the blade with my tongue. He carved out a hole big enough so that I could move my lips. I mouthed, "Why?"

My voice was so low it seemed like it belonged to someone far away.

"It's not complicated."

"You killed them all."

"You're funny. You're so fuckin' lost it's funny."

I thought, *I'll tell him I loved him.* Instead I said, "Bastard."

He slid back and rested his butt on my knees. He touched the bottom of my ribs and kissed my balls and ran his tongue along my cock.

"See, I love you too, sweetie."

"Jesus," I said. The pain made me turn away.

I thought I heard him say something about saving me for another run. I didn't understand. He wasn't making any sense. With the blunt end of the knife, he made small circles in the tape around my mouth.

"You don't hate me," I said.

"I don't hate anyone. I love killing." He cut more slits into the tape.

I tried to scream but my voice was ruined.

"No one can hear you. You're mine. I was hoping you would have made a move on me sometime this weekend. We could have made love and then this moment would have been even better. I like to imagine cutting someone who believes he loves me."

"Fuck you," I said.

"That's the bad man inside you talking trash, the one who hides in his secret life. Down deep, you feel sorry for me. You sensitive guys always do."

Then I felt the blade everywhere. He cut me behind my left ear, across my neck, made incisions in my chest, my thighs, the bend of my knees, my ankles, the bottom of my feet. The blood felt like water coursing over my body when I climbed out of the sea along a beach on a hot summer afternoon.

I reeled.

I dreamed of escape. He'd stop and leave me here before I lost so much strength I couldn't move. I'd crawl to the edge of the boathouse and reach my arm out just far enough so that someone would see my hand and call for help.

He said, "Now our secret lives converge."

I thought I heard a siren close by.

He took my chin in his hand and touched my lips with his tongue through a hole in the tape. I shuddered, and my vision blurred.

"I don't fit the profile, and that's why I'm not going to get caught."

He said something about Argentina and for a moment the whole space around me opened into a map of South America. He talked about an Argentine room, but he hadn't had time to capture the rats. He said the Argentine secret police were master sadists.

He pinned the condom to my chest. I smelled latex beneath the odor of blood.

He packed the knife inside the leather satchel. He remembered the gun and put it in too, hoisted the bag over his shoulder, looked at Lambert, unjammed the door of the boathouse, and walked out.

With him gone so inexplicably, the room no longer felt like a tomb. I heard wind whistling through the tall shore grasses. I managed to turn on my side—my body felt so heavy—and saw the river through the open door. Two long-legged terns stood on a rock and looked toward the boat-house. Maybe he'd startled them when he left. *They are our witnesses.*

Everything swam. I saw Sarah in my study. She was reading Jared's e-mail about the boathouse that I'd left on the screen. I saw her dialing 911. *He's slipped up. Soon the air along the riverbank would be swarming with police.*

I closed my eyes to stop the blurring and fought to keep from passing out. I heard Jamie singing "One is the Loneliest Number." I tried to respond, but I was frustrated because I couldn't get the lyrics right. She was standing on the riverbank and smiling the way she always did when she knew she had a song she could win with.

Jared didn't matter anymore. He wasn't there. Others joined my daughter on the bank. In the distance someone sang "Down By the River." Jamie smiled and wondered who these strange men were: Stephen Hart, with a pool stick in his hand, stood beside her. The young man with a Spiderman tattoo running down his arm waved a hankie in front of his face like he was a showgirl flirting with the camera. The detective appeared, without his faceless mask this time, but still in Army camouflage. Lambert—a boy really—lifted himself from the muck of the boathouse floor, walked out, and stood beside me. I looked around as if I was expecting, at any moment, something good to happen.

Acknowledgments

Friends can help a writer in ways they might not know. For their generosity I want to thank Barbara Fried, Erika Brigham, Sheldon Fried, Sarah Shepard, Rita Rogers, and Fritz and Sylvia Lahvis. I am especially grateful to two friends, Jim and Karen Shepard, who gave me piles of keen and invaluable advice. Years ago, at Notre Dame, Ernest and Eileen Sandeen gave me more kindness than a young man deserved. Thanks, too, to my fine editor, Nick Street, and Dan Cullinane and the other good people at Alyson.